Old Mrs. Kimble's Mansion

Other Books by George T. Arnold

Old Mrs. Kimble's Mansion
Wyandotte Bound

Old Mrs. Kimble's Mansion

George T. Arnold

SPEAKING VOLUMES, LLC
NAPLES, FLORIDA
2021

Old Mrs. Kimble's Mansion

Cover design by Hannah Linder

ISBN 978-1-64540-343-2

Dedication

To all family members, friends, colleagues, and former students proud to live in or be from West Virginia, where the mountains are majestic, and the people are neighborly.

Chapter One

A Curious Request
1985

"Well, I certainly wasn't expecting that," Mr. Vermillion utters as he hangs up his phone and steps into the outer office to share the news with Cassandra Pierce, his partner at their law firm on Stanford Avenue in downtown Asher Heights, West Virginia.

"Not expecting what, John?" Cassandra mumbles, her mind focused on her day's work schedule.

"A call with a curious request from a big-shot attorney at one of Chicago's most prestigious outfits."

"Oh?" Cassandra responds with a little more enthusiasm, sensing she could be about to hear something that might provide a break from the monotony in the daily routine of a couple of small-town lawyers.

"Get this, Cassandra. It seems someone who doesn't want us to know his identity is hiring us to buy the old Kimble mansion for him, and never anybody mind that it may not even be on the market."

"Fine with me," Cassandra answers without looking up from her papers, "but what if it's not for sale? What makes that Chicago lawyer representing 'Mr. Anonymous' think we, of all people, can buy it? We're not even in the real estate business."

"To me, that's the challenging part, my friend. That and the mysterious nature of the request. 'Money's no object!' " she said. "In fact, she said it twice.

"The guy is so dead set on having that mansion, its condition is no barrier either. And what's more, he's sending us a five-thousand-dollar retainer this afternoon!"

"Well, whoop-de-doo," Cassandra responds sarcastically. "Five thousand whole dollars? C'mon, John, there's no way you'd be this giddy over that amount of money. What gives?"

"Oh, just a fifty-thousand-dollar bonus if we can persuade the owners to sell within the next two weeks. Tell me that's not enough to get even your skeptical little heart pumping, Cassandra. So, you as ready as I am to get this adventure started?"

"Five figures does have a way of getting a gal's attention!" she concedes, dropping the papers she had been carefully organizing as if they were so many used napkins. "How 'bout doing a drive by right now? We have an hour before we have to be in court."

"I'm game. Your car or mine?"

***

Unknown to John Vermillion, the offbeat phone call was set in motion by an old acquaintance from his high school graduation class of 1959. Someone he has not seen or even thought about in more than twenty years.

"I knew I had my surrogate as soon as I checked out the list of Asher Heights lawyers and saw John's name," Forrest Alderson explains, sitting in the Chicago office of his primary attorney, Olivia Fillmore, who possesses a law degree from Yale, a Phi Beta Kappa key, and head-turner beauty.

"John wasn't one of my run-around friends, but he was one of the best of the good guys I grew up with," Forrest assures Olivia. "And I picked you to handle things for me because I trust you more than anybody else in this overpriced law empire I've been paying a fortune in retainer fees all these years."

"Appreciate that, Forrest," the fashionably slender Olivia responds, uncrossing her pretty long legs and leaning forward in her chair, touching his forearm to indicate she is personally concerned about Forrest and his astonishing lifestyle change.

"But what I don't get is why at forty-four you've sold one of the most successful real estate firms in Chicago to retire back to your home town of Nowheresville when you haven't stepped foot in the place since you were shaving fuzz off your face.

"And what in the hell do you want with an old mansion that, for all you know, may be dilapidated and overrun with raccoons and squirrels and Lord knows what all else you West Virginians have lurking in those hills you hold so precious?

"In the three years I've known you, Forrest, you've never once mentioned that old place."

"Well, seeing as how you brought it up—and considering I'm not paying one thin dime for this conversation—I'll tell you about it. And I want you to know," he winks, "you can feel privileged because you'll be the first to hear something I've never said out loud even to myself."

"I'm all ears," she retorts, more annoyed than amused by his cavalier attitude, and once again irritated by his apparent inability to notice her subtle attempts to flirt with him. She scoots to the back of her chair and crosses her legs again, showing a bit more thigh than she otherwise would if she were not attracted to him.

Oblivious as usual, Forrest begins his explanation. "Olivia, as far back as I can remember, that big mansion on Rhododendron Ridge belonged to a woman known as Old Mrs. Kimble. And I don't say that disrespectfully; that's what everybody called her. I never knew her first name, and neither did any of my buddies. We figured it wasn't 'Old,' but we never heard anything else.

"Funny thing, none of us actually ever saw her either. We were told she'd become a very young widow when her husband was killed during the Spanish-American War. Folks say that forever after that, she secluded herself in that huge house, sometime around the turn of the century."

"As young and as rich as she was, she never got married again, Forrest?"

"Nope. Never so much as looked romantically at another man, or so I'm told, Olivia. And there must have been all kinds of suitors—sincere ones, as well as fortune hunters. But she spurned every one of them.

"I sort of got acquainted with the mansion and the stories about Old Mrs. Kimble because her next-door neighbors were the Rutherfords, and their son Whitney was one of my best friends. Actually, I was lucky to have him for a friend because the Rutherfords had money, unlike my family and most of the other guys Whitney and I ran around with.

"His dad could afford to build a hard-surface basketball court near the long line of hedges that separated their property from the mansion. And Whitney's parents didn't seem to mind having a bunch of us boys hanging around playing ball four or five days out of the week.

"We practically lived on that court from the fourth grade through high school. Except when it snowed, and it did a lot of that in Asher Heights, West Virginia."

"Got it, Forrest. You had a friend who had a basketball court, and it snows a lot in West Virginia. Think you might get around to telling me about the house anytime in the near future?"

"Well, don't you get surly when you're not getting paid, Olivia! Never noticed you being so antsy when I'm forking over hundreds of dollars an hour for you to listen. Keep your drawers on, as we West Virginians say; I'm getting to it.

"I couldn't miss looking at the house because the basketball goal faced its east side. And it was so big and fancy I couldn't help being impressed. So, if you can quit squirming long enough, I'll describe it to you in some detail."

"I'm listening. See!" she exclaims, pushing her ears out horizontally with the palms of her hands.

"Then picture this, Miss Impatient: The mansion sat about a hundred yards from the street, and the big woods in back stretched all the way to McDowell Road, which runs parallel to Rhododendron Ridge. Not counting the full-sized underground basement, it stood two tall stories high with the first floor about ten feet above street level.

"What I liked best by far were the massive round white columns that started at the base of the wrap-around porch and peaked at the level of the attic. I felt like a pygmy the first time I saw them!

"The rest consisted of walls formed from thousands of white bricks with squishy mortar of the same color bulging out between them. The bricks surrounded giant oak double doors and a bunch of tall windows and shutters.

"You couldn't see through them though, and believe me we tried. They were mostly hidden by telephone-pole-tall juniper trees. And Old Mrs. Kimble kept all of her draperies and curtains closed to keep us and everybody else from peeking in on her. So, obviously, we never got inside either, which led us boys to imagine the house possessed every-thing from secret treasures to some other really creepy stuff.

"You following me so far, Olivia?"

"Oh, yeah. I'm almost getting curious. Get on with it before I turn middle-aged."

Forrest was tempted to remind her that forty is middle-aged. But you just don't say that sort of thing to any woman, particularly a good-looking one who has the self-image of a twenty-something.

"Anyway, Oliva, even though I was pretty young, that vision of a rich person's home found a permanent place in my memory. You see, my family lived from paycheck to paycheck, so all I could do was daydream about a lot of the things I wanted but couldn't have, even imagining someday being master of that awesome house.

"But the thought was so foolish, I kept it to myself until today. I mean, what could I envision as a boy that I could do short of robbery to put enough money together to buy an estate so fine? It wasn't like I could count on inheriting a family fortune or becoming a big movie star, or anything as unlikely as that.

"Anyhow, it became an obsession never far from my thoughts, even now, more than three decades later."

"OK, I understand the attraction, Forrest; it sounds both fabulous and a little mysterious. But, for Heaven's sake, you've been filthy rich for quite a while. Why haven't you been back home to see it and to visit your old friends? You could have bought that place a long time ago, hired a caretaker and visited whenever you had the time or the inclination. Doesn't make sense to me."

"I suppose it doesn't, Olivia. But the reasons are painfully personal. Something else I've kept to myself."

"I'm a good listener Forrest; that is, when I'm interested. And now that you finally have my full attention, I'd almost pay you to find out. Almost that is," she says with a cute mock smile that usually works wonders on the male gender but doesn't seem to faze Forrest.

"Seriously, I'm willing to step back into the attorney-client privilege relationship—off the clock, of course—if you want to confide in me. Goes without saying, I'll keep the information confidential."

"I'm tempted to tell you, Olivia. It's not something I'd ever feel comfortable talking about with a man, or not even with many women for that matter. But you're smart and you're insightful and a good enough friend, I think, to put yourself in my place and see all the complexities from my point of view.

"Sure you want to hear this?"

"Truthfully, Forrest, I'm damned eager. Talk all you want. I'm turning off my phones, and I promise I'll keep my mouth shut until you make it crystal clear you want to hear from me. Cross my heart."

"OK, Olivia," Forrest begins, a troubled expression overtaking the features of his usually pleasant face. "It started with a personal tragedy that happened when I was twenty-one. That put an abrupt end to my daydreaming about the kind of life I wanted and forced me to face the hard fact that a person makes his or her own future.

"So, I set a goal of earning as much money as I could as fast as I could, and I dedicated myself totally and solely to that end. Believe me, the road I've traveled all these years is paved with money. Nothing else."

Judging a look of earnest interest from Olivia, Forrest plunges on while the gate to his secret past is still ajar. "In the twenty-three years since then, I've become enormously wealthy. But you know all of that. All of my finances are recorded in your company's books.

"You know I made my fortune in Chicago real estate by buying and selling so many expensive houses and high-rise buildings that I can't remember half of them. And I invested almost everything I cleared. Spent damned little on myself, such as places to live, cars, clothes, vacations—any of the things rich people usually splurge on.

"Anyway, a couple of years ago, I decided I had made more than enough money to let me liquidate a bunch of my holdings, move back home and buy that mansion I've been set on having all these years.

"I kept that decision to myself, and, honestly, that was a hard thing to do because the time between then and now has dragged out like the poky period between Thanksgiving and Christmas does when you're a kid. But, finally, with the phone call you made to John Vermillion this morning, my goal is in sight, and I'm itching to get it done."

"Forrest, I know I promised just to listen, but you seem to have forgotten I have no clue what 'The Tragedy' is. How do you expect me to understand until you tell me what happened to get all this started? And you haven't told me whether you know for sure that old mansion is even still there."

"You're right; I'm presuming too much. Sorry. Let me explain it this way. I have my own reasons for not knowing for sure whether it's still standing or it's a pile of bricks. I know how weird that sounds, but the truth is I did not want to know because that would have taken away the second biggest driving force I had for building my fortune. The other reason is the tragedy—the most tormenting experience in my life, and an even bigger motivator.

"You see, I haven't been back to my hometown since right after I graduated from college. My family moved to the West Coast during my junior year, and the last time I was in Asher Heights was to get married.

"Yeah, Olivia, you can shut your mouth now and get that shocked look off your face. You heard right; I did say married. Hard to believe coming from a middle-aged bachelor who runs like hell anytime any woman even hints she is romantically interested."

"As if I didn't know!" Olivia wanted to say out loud but clamped down on her tongue.

"Anyway, Maggie McDaniel Mullens and I had been engaged unofficially since high school and officially since the Christmas before I finished college. She was gorgeous, Olivia, and sexy as hell. I was so hopelessly, helplessly, achingly in love with her, it was like being hooked on a narcotic.

"She came from a good family, too, although I was a little put off by her somewhat goofy mother who had a bunch of silly hangups like giving all of her children names that started with the same letter: Maggie McDaniel, Mason McGeorge, and Millicent Marie. All of their clothes had three capital M's monogrammed glaringly on them, and her mother couldn't understand why each of my names, Forrest Walker Alderson, started with a different letter. I told her to blame it on my parents who apparently liked trees.

"I hadn't seen much of Maggie and her family during my final Spring semester. I was too busy trying to graduate with honors while working part time and sending out resumes to companies I hoped would hire me. Maggie already had graduated from another university in December and was busy planning our wedding . . . ."

When his voice unexpectedly breaks, betraying the matter-of-fact manner in which he was forcing himself to tell his tale, he hesitates, coughs a couple of times, struggling to regain control.

After an embarrassing interval, he manages to continue. "Or so I believed. Until exactly one week before the wedding when she abruptly threw me over and, like some kind of traitor, deserted me and our plans for a future together. We'd already sent out invitations, made all the arrangements, and spent a lot a of non-refundable money.

"Worse, everyone in town including all my boyhood and college friends and their families became aware of the scandalous details. Believe me, Olivia, it would have been kinder of Maggie if she had shot bullets into me instead of words that permanently scarred my heart and screwed me up where romance is concerned."

"Oh, I am so very sorry, Forrest," Olivia interjects, unable to keep herself from interrupting, but gaining some insight into why he has never acted on her implied advances.

"I don't want you to be sorry, Olivia. I want you to understand.

"Maggie's reason enraged even her own family and deeply embarrassed them before the entire community. The hell of it is, Maggie didn't simply get cold feet; she tossed me aside for one of those edgy bad-boy types so many otherwise sensible females at one time or another in their lives go nuts over; intoxicated, I suppose, by their misguided notions of sex appeal and excited by the potential danger these no-goods represent. But foolishly blind to these perpetual adolescents' lack of responsibility, ambition, and conscience.

"LeRoy Bottoms, that dimwit Maggie fell for, dropped out of school so unscathed by education he couldn't tell a double negative in a sentence from a double dribble on a basketball court. His underfed brain was so empty, he couldn't form a sentence that didn't start with 'OK' and end with 'yuh know what I'm sayin'?' "

Forrest shakes his head like a dog flinging water off its coat, apparently still unable to grasp why Maggie, or any other female with a lick of sense, could fall for such a loser.

"Some gullible females, like Maggie, even marry these predators," Forrest says with palpable bitterness. "More often than not after becoming pregnant, as she did. About which time, Mr. Edgy loses interest and preys on some other dreamy-eyed female convinced beyond all reason he loves *only her,* and she is *The One* who can change him."

"Did you confront them?" Olivia interrupts.

"Hell no. She made it clear there was nothing I could do to change her mind. So, I slinked out of Asher Heights after dark that same night and never looked back. Never went back. Not even for a high school class reunion. I cut off contact with everyone, including my lifelong best friends.

"Olivia, can you understand it wasn't simply that I was embarrassed; I was so heartsick and humiliated, I seriously considered suicide. Or murder. Or both.

"I truly believed for a time I'd go crazy trying to force out of my mind the vision of my Maggie eagerly giving her beautiful body to someone so undeserving and so unappreciative. That image was—and all these years later remains—torturous."

Olivia's disciplined attention is redirected by a couple of tears that manage to escape her eyes, slowly trickling past her mouth before she can turn sideways and wipe them away. Fortunately, Forrest doesn't see them. The shame he has felt all these years has kept him from looking directly at Olivia.

"But somehow, after agonizing for several days, I managed to create a purpose for going on. I convinced myself I would live to someday show Maggie she'd made the biggest mistake of her life. Call it revenge; call it getting even; call it whatever you like. I just knew I wanted Maggie to feel the depth of suffering she put me through.

"How? I did not know. When? I had no clue. But sometime.

"To this day, as you know, Olivia, I have never married. No woman, I am convinced, is worth the risk of going through such excruciating pain again. Instead, I substituted work for love. That's all I existed for. I lived cheaply and invested my money wisely. Extraordinarily wisely, I can say now without boasting."

Olivia does know how he has lived. And for the first time, she is beginning to understand why.

"Except for a little hiking by myself on weekends, all I did was work. But my work and my investments paid off. And, by damn, I made it big. After all those years dedicated almost exclusively to making money, I'm worth millions upon millions!

"I think I can go back home almost anonymously now because I doubt anyone in Asher Heights knows anything about my adult life or my wealth. Why should they? Not even my parents and my two siblings suspect I have more than a few million dollars, although I've treated them very generously."

"If you've treated them so 'generously,' " Olivia silently asks herself, "why haven't they somehow intervened in your lonely, tortured life? Guess you wouldn't let them," she concedes.

11

"Chances are no one in my hometown will even recognize me. After all, I'm middle-aged, what used to be my dark brown hair is at least half gray, and, as you can see, I've recently grown a short beard, and I like it. On top of that, I've bought an old Chevrolet sedan no one would look at twice. I'm betting nobody will notice me.

"So, until I have John Vermillion working through you to purchase the mansion for me, I'll be incognito in Asher Heights. By then, my investigators and I should have discovered everything I want to know: Who's who, who's where, and who's doing what. Including Maggie McDaniel Mullens whatever-the-hell-her-last-name-is-now."

"Oh, Forrest, what a perfectly horrid experience. I mean, I've been through a divorce and a couple of other painful breakups in my time, but nothing that affected me like yours has. But, please, because you've trusted me enough to confide in me, I'll intrude on your privacy just enough to ask you a couple of questions I pray you've already carefully considered."

"Go ahead, Olivia. I'd like to know what you're thinking."

"First, Forrest, are you willing to spend perhaps several million dollars to buy and restore that old mansion because you really want to live in it? Or is it because you want to rub your great wealth and success in Maggie's face and show her what a terrible mistake she made? If revenge is your reason, I fear for you, my friend. I truly do."

"Obvious questions, Olivia, and of course, I've considered them. Many times. The raw truth is I do not know for sure. I'm aware of the possible consequences and all that. But it's something I've got to do, and I'll only find out the truth by actually doing it."

"Then God go with you," Olivia says, rising from her chair and surprising Forrest with a hug so intimate that even he couldn't mistake its meaning.

Chapter Two

Return to Asher Heights

Old Mrs. Kimble's mansion is still standing.

But not by much.

John and Cassandra can plainly see from her car the faded shutters, the decaying porch, the missing roofing tiles, and the neglected lawn. They can only speculate on what the inside looks like.

"Oh, my goodness," Cassandra sighs. "I had no idea the old place was in such sad shape. Makes me wonder if 'Mr. Anonymous' will even want it when he sees it. Best we discreetly take some pictures and send them to his lawyer."

"I agree," John says. "After court I'll come back with my camera. The man's lawyer distinctly said 'no matter what kind of shape it's in,' but I want to check to make sure before we try to contact the owners."

***

Forrest was dead serious when he assured the lawyers he wanted the mansion no matter its condition. So he wastes no time on the eight-hour drive from Chicago to the Ohio River bridge leading into Huntington, West Virginia, the second largest city in the state and home of Marshall University, a school for which Forrest formed a strong fondness when he was a teenager.

There was nothing along the way he particularly wanted to see until getting to West Virginia, where he would spend the night in Huntington and revisit some of the places he first saw when he was fifteen years old and had pestered his parents into allowing him to go with friends to the state basketball tournament.

Asher Heights High School lost in the semifinal round, but that didn't completely spoil the trip. After seeing the Marshall campus—and especially after getting a jaw-dropping look at scores of pretty coeds—Forrest determined he would enroll there after high school, visiting several times before he graduated. But finances dictated otherwise. A scholarship combined with a work opportunity took him in another direction in the state to a smaller college.

"Good Lord, I'm almost three times as old now as I was then," Forrest muses. "I thought I was in a really big city, what with all the four-lane avenues running parallel to one another and numbered instead of having names like our streets in Asher Heights. Had its own station for passenger trains instead of our locomotives that just carried coal. Even had those big city Checker Marathon taxicabs."

It's no surprise to Forrest, but still unrealistically disappointing, that Huntington isn't the same place anymore. Marshall has developed from a college into a university with a much bigger enrollment even though a loss of manufacturing jobs has led to a decrease in the city's population, and the place doesn't seem so big after he's lived in Chicago for a quarter of a century.

Forrest drives east on Fifth Avenue, slowing as he passes by the south side of the university. The new buildings give the campus a considerably different appearance, and he notices with a little sadness that Yawkey Student Union, with its constantly playing jukebox and large dance floor, is no more.

"Wonder if students dance as much in that new center?" he asks himself. Every young person in southern West Virginia was a good dancer during the jitterbug era, Forrest remembers, still a little annoyed that singer Chubby Checker introduced some contortionistic maneuver called the twist that eventually pushed jitterbugging aside. "Hated the twist then and still do," he grumbles. "What kind of dance requires people to grind their feet as if they were putting out burning cigarettes?"

He drives about ten more blocks to get a sentimental look at Memorial Field House where he and his friends saw Asher Heights play in the state tournament all those years ago. "Still looks about the same," he's glad to see.

Forrest feels something of a loss as he recalls how exciting it was to be in that building with eight thousand screaming fans sitting so close to the court, they could almost reach out and touch the players. "Took it all for granted back then. Just as I did a whole bunch of other things I'll never have the chance to live over again."

Forrest turns left on Twenty-Ninth Street, gets a good view of ever-expanding St. Mary's Hospital, and takes a left on Third Avenue, heading to the north side of campus and some of the students' favorite hangouts, especially The El Gato where he first heard Roy Orbison's "Only the Lonely," a song that still conjures up faded images of college life and all those coeds in the prime of their beauty and sensuality.

He wants to use the remaining half hour of daylight to drive by some pretty homes on the South Side of Huntington. Beautiful Ritter Park is still much the same, and the stately houses are as impressive as ever. The large one provided for the president of Marshall University faces the park and is quite elegant.

Three of Forrest's favorite eating places remain in business—Stewart's Original Hot Dogs made precisely the same way for generations, Cam's Ham continuing to produce the best baked ham sandwiches in the universe, and Jim's Steak and Spaghetti House, a regular stop not only for Huntingtonians but also for celebrities passing through town.

"Thank God they haven't changed," he takes in with a rush of nostalgia, eating at two of the places and getting a to-go order at the third to carry him through the rest of the trip.

He drives south on Interstate 64 early the next morning, passing through Charleston, the state's capital and largest city. It was there at age ten he first rode an escalator. That was in the Diamond Department Store, close to where he window-shopped at upscale Frankenberger's men's clothing. He couldn't afford anything either offered, and now that he has more than enough money to buy both stores and every single item in them, they no longer exist.

As he drives through the city, he catches a glimpse out the passenger side window of the spectacular capitol and is reminded again that its gold-leaf dome is the grandest he's ever seen. A picture of it was on the front inside cover of his ninth-grade civics book, and Forrest always felt proud knowing that text was being used by students all over the United States.

Three hours' distance from Huntington, he exits into New River County where Asher Heights is located and enters the lobby of Grand Overlook Resort.

"I trust you will find the accommodations to your liking, sir," Mr. Farnsmill recites in rote repetition as he hands Forrest the key to the small log cabin he is renting at the resort, a six-thousand-acre wooded site Mr. Farnsmill and his family own and operate. The tree-sheltered, out-of-the-way location affords the privacy Forrest wants, and as a bonus he had not thought about, it is rustic and beautiful.

He registers under the name of Bret Doyle, not wanting to reveal his identity until the time is right. He chooses Bret because that's what he would have named himself if he had possessed the powers of speech and persuasion when he was born. Doyle comes from his love of that author's Sherlock Holmes stories.

193

```
|||||||||||||||||||||||||||||||||||
```
58CV3Y000176

missing pages. The spine/binding may show signs of wear and, while the majority of pages are undamaged, same may have notes, highlighting, small tears, and/or creasing. The cover art image is a stock photo; the actual cover may have slight sticky residue and there may be a "From the Library Of" label or previous owner's name inside. Additional materials (e.g. access codes, discs, tables, charts, cards, letters, etc.) may not be included. Fast Shipping Monday through Friday - Safe and Secure! Please verify your shipping address at time of purchase to ensure delivery.

"So far, so good," Forrest figures, expecting to hear from Olivia any moment about John Vermillion's initial contact with the mansion's owners. Waiting patiently, however, is not among Forrest's most praiseworthy traits, so he unpacks quickly, gets back into his old sedan and heads to town, determined to reacquaint himself with every street, alley, and highway.

Chapter Three

"It's Not for Sale"

"Louisa, there's some lawyer wanting to talk to you on the phone. I told him you're eating brunch and to state his business. But he's determined to discuss buying our house and insists on talking to you because you're the owner."

"Did you tell him it's not up for sale, Alistair?" she shouts from the kitchen table.

"Sure I did. But he says the offer will be too good not to at least listen to."

"Oh, all right. But what he wants with a run-down old mansion I'm sure I don't know," she fusses, pulling her worn housecoat together in front and reluctantly leaving the table and her hot meal.

Taking the phone, Louisa says with obvious irritation, "This is Louisa Malcolmson. Who is this?"

"Hello, Mrs. Malcolmson. This is John Vermillion of the law firm of Vermillion and Pierce. You may remember me; we used to attend the same church a few years back."

"Yeah, John, I know you. My husband said something about your wanting to buy our house. You know it's not for sale, don't you? We haven't even been considering such a thing."

"I realize that, Mrs. Malcolmson. But I have a client who's very interested. He acquired my services to determine if you'd be willing to have the house appraised—at his expense, of course—and let him make an offer. You have nothing to lose, and I can assure you this man is serious and can afford to pay cash."

"Who is this man, John? And, by the way, call me Louisa. Everybody else does."

"Thank you, Louisa. For now, he wants to remain anonymous. Fact is, I don't know who he is myself and haven't even spoken to him. One of his lawyers from a big city firm authorized me to make the inquiry. But I can guarantee this man is on the level and his offer will be legitimate.

"Frankly, my partner, Cassandra Pierce, and I are as curious as we can be to find out who he is and what his connection is to Asher Heights. So, what do you say, Louisa. May I drop by tomorrow and talk with you? The worst that could happen is you get a free inspection and an appraisal with a complete list of the positives and negatives of your house."

"I'll think on it, John. I need time to take it all in; this is a little too sudden for me. I'll get back to you if I have a mind to."

"Of course. But I'd appreciate it if you'd let me call you day after tomorrow. The potential buyer is truly very, very eager."

"You don't say, John. Well, then, if he's all that smitten with the place, let me ask you one question. As you know, this house has been in my family since it was built in the 1890s. I am a direct descendant of Old Mrs. Kimble from my mother's side of the family and damned proud of it. So, let's be clear up front. The mansion is not in the condition we would want it to be, but it means a lot to us all the same.

"That means I do not want to get myself and my husband all worked up only to have your man try to buy the place at a bargain-basement price. Let him know we won't even sell at market value, if we sell at all. What he says to that will determine if I am willing to move ahead."

"Appreciate your candor, Louisa. I'll do that right away. But I guarantee you can count on him saying yes. My word on it."

Chapter Four

Bret Doyle Inspects the "Old Lady"

"Oh, dear God, I can't believe I'm here and it's here," Forrest almost gasps as he takes his first look in a quarter of a century at Old Mrs. Kimble's mansion. Feeling lightheaded as his heart races, he momentarily forgets he might be overheard by the local building inspector and the appraiser accompanying him.

"What's that yuh say?" Barney Summerfield, the construction expert, asks, spraying the lawn with tobacco juice from the ever-present wad of Mail Pouch tucked into his left cheek. Barney heard Forrest speak but not clearly enough to understand what he said.

"Oh, nothing worth repeating, Barney. I was just remarking to myself how awesome this old mansion is despite its rundown condition. I just hope the inside is in better shape."

But it is not.

Posing as Bret Doyle, ostensibly a representative of the potential buyer, Forrest steps through the front door with Barney, and Calvin Quesenberry, the appraiser, and immediately the ravages of time and neglect register vividly in their minds. The once beautiful wooden floors and walls are dull and faded; the imported rugs are threadbare in more places than not; wallpaper is peeling; and the entire house has the musty smell of trapped air.

"Hope thuh man thinkin' about buyin' this house has deep pockets," Barney whispers to the other two. "Puttin' this place back into prime condition is gonna cost a right smart amount of money."

"We won't know for sure until we give it a good going over," Calvin chimes in. "But if the roof, the plumbing, and the electrical system are as bad as these few rooms we've already seen, a thorough renovation will definitely run into the six figures. Maybe seven."

As straight-faced as the three men try to be in hiding their shock, their first reaction is read all too clearly by Louisa and Alistair, neither of whom is surprised.

"I told that lawyer, John Vermillion, the kind of condition the 'Old Lady' is in," Louisa offers, determined to make sure the men know she is honest and is holding nothing back.

"You're welcome to look it over from top to bottom. Take all the time you like. Alistair and I are interested in knowing what fixing the place up would cost and what it's worth as it stands now. You got any questions, just holler."

"Thank you, Mrs. Malcolmson," Forrest replies. "I'm sure we will have questions later on. Meanwhile," he says, looking at his companions, "what do you say we get started?"

***

The inspection takes three hours in the morning, followed by two more after a break for lunch. By the time they finish, Forrest, Calvin, and Barney look as if they have been mining coal, except they are smudged and smeared with brown dirt and dust instead of the deep black coating miners have at the end of their shift.

"Can't help feelin' sorry deep down in my soul," Barney reveals as they are leaving. "If a buildin' could have feelin's, this grand Old Lady would be embarrassed plumb tuh death over thuh way she looks. Nobody who cares a hoot about thuh history of this place wudda let it go down like this unless they didn't have the money tuh keep it up. Shudda sold it long ago to somebody who could."

Eager to have at least a guesstimate of the value of the mansion and what it would cost to restore it, Forrest asks Barney his thinking.

"Well, for sure it needs just about everything—roof, plumbin', electrical, heatin', central air, refinishin' of thuh floors and walls, rebuildin' thuh collapsed ceilin's in two of thuh unused bedrooms, competely new bathrooms and kitchen . . . Damn near ever'thing," Barney calculates, a staggering cost taking shape in his mind. "We're definitely talkin' about seven figures tuh do a top-notch job of it."

"How about a preliminary appraisal, Calvin?" Forrest requests.

"Don't hold me to this, Bret, but I think my estimate will be in the ballpark. If it were in top condition, I think its value in this part of the country would be about five million dollars. In its current shape, no more than one and a half million. Probably less. What's your thinking, Bret?"

"In an upscale section of a big city like Chicago, I'd say about fifteen million in top condition. As is, about five million."

"Think thuh guy wantin' tuh buy it will still want it after he gets our report?" Barney asks.

"We'll see, Barney. I'll let both of you know. But in the meantime, I'll caution you again that our involvement must be kept among ourselves until our man makes up his mind."

What Forrest withholds from Barney and Calvin, in addition to his real identity, is that "the man" has never wavered in his determination to possess Old Mrs. Kimble's mansion. No matter its current condition or anything else. In fact, Forrest is more determined than ever because of something he was stunned to see in the mansion's main room.

In his mind's eye, he had always pictured Mrs. Kimble as an old woman because she was in her late seventies when he first saw the mansion. But the portrait of her over the grand fireplace shocks him to his core. The painting reveals a young, vivacious, and extraordinarily beautiful woman.

"I'll be damned," he mutters. "I'll just be damned!" he says out loud with force.

"If there ever was such a thing as a one-man woman, she must have been it, shutting herself up in this place the way she did for almost a lifetime. My goodness, with her beauty, her wealth, and her position in the community, there's no doubt she could have had her pick of men," Forrest reasons.

"I've got to have that portrait along with the house and leave it where it has been since the mansion was built. It would be a sacrilege to do otherwise."

Chapter Five

An Offer "They Can't Turn Down"

"I overheard part of what those men were saying during the inspection, Louisa, and if their judgment is accurate, the Old Lady is in even worse condition than we thought."

"How so, Alistair?"

"The long and the short of it, my dear, is the place is literally falling down around us. The roof is so rotten, it's about to collapse on our heads. The one called Barney, who builds and inspects houses for a living, said the roof already is leaking into two second-floor bedrooms, and at least a big section of it could fall anytime."

"Dang, Alistair. I just hate to face up to this. Guess I've been hoping against hope the place would outlast us. Lord knows we've gone twenty years or more without the money to take proper care of it. But that doesn't make it any easier for me to come to grips with selling it."

"I understand, Louisa, and I feel the same way. But if we don't sell while it's still restorable, we could end up with nothing but land we can't afford to rebuild on. Then how would we live? Seriously!"

"Did you hear them say what they think the mansion is worth, Alistair?"

"No. Wish I had, but I didn't."

"Any guess about what we can get for it?"

"No, Louisa. I just know if it were in top condition, the mansion and the land would be worth millions. As is, I'd be very happy to get more than a million. Could be more because the land has not only held its value, it has appreciated, I'm sure."

"OK, Alistair. We have to be smart. We owe a lot of money, but we still have enough credit to hire our own appraiser to make sure the crew here today doesn't try to lowball us. When the potential buyer makes an offer, I want to know what is realistic. I've already made clear we won't sell for the appraised value. Although now that we know how bad things are, I figure all we can do is use that statement as a bluff."

Alistair offers to get a friend, Mary Anne Craycraft, to agree to a hurry up meeting. "We can trust her to give us sound financial-planning advice about how much we'll need to live comfortably for the rest of our lives. If we can get enough out of the house for that, parting with the Old Lady will be a whole lot easier to live with."

***

True to his word, Forrest determines to pay more for the mansion than its market value. For several reasons. First, he knows the Malcolmsons do not want to part with it. They love the house; it has always been in their family; and they are not immune to the prestige living there gives them in the community. Regardless of its condition, the Old Lady confers instant status upon its inhabitants. Forrest will have to pay for that as much or moreso than for the land and the physical structure.

"Besides," he insists to himself, "they deserve whatever they can get.

I'm asking them, in effect, to be the generation that cost their family their mansion. Their heritage, really. And that's asking a lot of anyone."

He and Calvin and Barney settle on an appraised value of a million and a half. That will not be enough to satisfy the Malcolmsons, Forrest knows, although he could risk pressuring them into accepting that amount before the place falls under its own weight and becomes virtually worthless.

"Wouldn't be fair, and besides, I won't take that risk. I'll make them an offer they can't turn down."

Forrest puts together a package that includes two million dollars for the mansion and the property, a new American luxury car of their choice, and a buy-in at Mountaineer Manor, the finest retirement resort in the area. It offers a far better lifestyle than the Malcolmsons have in their mansion: a three hundred thousand dollar house or condo; all meals when they prefer to eat in the restaurant instead of preparing their own food in their fully equipped kitchen; a complete schedule of social and recreational activities; a country club with golf, tennis, and swimming facilities; group trips ranging from a day to more than a week; a medical clinic with an assisted-living unit; twenty-four-hour chauffeur service; salons to meet every personal grooming need; a laundry; professional shoppers, and many other amenities.

Altogether, the package Forrest's agents, John Vermillion and Cassandra Pierce, will offer amounts to two and a half million dollars.

Forrest gives John and Cassandra the go-ahead, sits back more anxiously and impatiently than he would like, and waits to find out if he finally is going to realize a dream he has been working toward his entire adult life.

***

Less than an hour into their tour of Mountaineer Manor, Louisa and Alistair look each other in the eye and nod, sometimes the only communication necessary between a man and a woman who have shared their lives for more than half a century.

"We will be happy here, won't we, Alistair?" Louisa asks wistfully.

"Darned right, Louisa. It's a beautiful place. It has everything we need and much more, and we'll never lack for the company of people in our own age group. I'm ready to move in tomorrow."

"Well," Louisa laughs, her husband's enthusiasm lifting her own, "we might need a smidgen more time than that. But not long. Now that we've decided to sell, I don't want to linger any longer than necessary. It hurts my heart to give up the place, but we have no choice, so let's go ahead and pick out a house or a condo. They're all luxurious; we can't go wrong no matter which we choose."

"Fine, Louisa. You pick. I'll be happy with whatever you want. And on the way home, let's stop at the Cadillac dealer, and I'll select the car and the color. Fair enough?"

"Fair enough, my dear."

"Oh, guess we'd best call John and Cassandra before we go to spending all this money, Louisa."

"Right, Alistair. And don't forget the stipulation we want in return for that last-minute request from the buyer."

Forrest had Olivia instruct his attorneys—who are thrilled with their fifty-thousand-dollar bonus and being placed on retainer—to ask if he can keep the portrait of Old Mrs. Kimble over the mantel. Figuring the mansion should always be identified with her, the Malcolmsons concur, asking in return to be invited to visit after the restoration. Forrest, through his lawyers, readily agrees. He wants very much to know they approve.

Chapter Six

Olivia's Pretext for a Visit

As Olivia's plane lands at Yeager Airport in Charleston, she is mindful the trip is totally unnecessary. She could have read Forrest the investigators' report over the phone or sent it to him any number of other ways. But she is curious, and, besides, she is paying her own expenses, and although it annoys her to admit it, she is eager to be with him.

"Whether Forrest likes it or not, I'm going to see Old Mrs. Kimble's mansion as it is now, so I can fully appreciate what it takes to look the way it will when the renovations are finished. Considering all the time I'm putting into assisting him while he's doing all of this, maybe he'll even let me help decorate it."

As she walks through the terminal to the rental car area, Olivia notices the tributes to the man for whom the airport is named: Brigadier General Chuck Yeager, a native West Virginian and a flying legend who is the first person to pilot an airplane faster than the speed of sound.

"I've heard of him, of course," she mentions to an elderly man who also stopped to read about the World War II hero. "Good to know he's from West Virginia."

"Yes, indeed," the man says. "We're right proud to claim him as one of our own."

Olivia rents a Ford Mustang, checks her AAA map and heads toward Asher Heights. She is still mulling over whether to set Forrest in a chair by his log cabin fireplace and, tossing aside the subtlety that has so far gotten her nowhere, tell him in language he cannot possibly misinterpret exactly how she feels about him.

If he reacts favorably and their relationship moves to a romantic level, wonderful; if not, she has less to lose now that he has moved back to West Virginia permanently. Whether she does nothing or she confronts him, and he rejects her, he'll still be in West Virginia and she'll be in Chicago.

"It's worth a shot," she convinces herself.

Olivia arrives at Forrest's one-story lodging in Grand Overlook Resort, and after accepting a soft drink West Virginians call "pop," she sits with Forrest in chairs facing the large window that provides a clear view of the woods.

"Why didn't you tell me how beautiful West Virginia is, Forrest? You know I'm a big city girl, and I've never been here before. Gosh, if the hills are this magnificent while the trees' leaves are green, I can only imagine what a riot of color Fall must bring on."

"Oh yeah, Olivia. The scenery here at home is spectacular. Guess we West Virginians grow so accustomed to it, we too often take it for granted."

"Well, you shouldn't, Forrest. Chicago has many wonders to experience, as you know from living there almost twenty-five years, but this is so very different for me. My only disappointment is that I don't have the sensation of being high up in the mountains. I thought I'd seem to be on top of the world in your state."

"Say, Olivia, you've given me an idea for a little trip, if you can stay another day and fly back Monday. Will your schedule allow that?"

"If I can get back to my office by noon Monday, I can stay. What do you have in mind?"

"We can get to that after a while, Olivia. Right now, if you aren't too tired, let's take a walk in the woods, so you can get a little feel for what life is like in a rural part of the country."

"Fine. I'd love to. Give me fifteen minutes to change into something more appropriate, and I'll be ready to roam the hills with you. Any chance we'll come across a moonshine still?" she jokes.

"You'll know we have if someone starts shooting at us," he teases.

Before they've walked half a mile among the pines whose aroma reminds her of Christmas trees, they spot a doe and two yearlings, several squirrels playing a game of chase, a couple of chipmunks, and more birds than Olivia can count.

"Boy, I wish I could step out of my Chicago office on one of my hectic days and escape to these woods for even a fifteen-minute break, Forrest. I bet my blood pressure and my heart rate have both dropped a load since we started walking. How peaceful. No, that's not the word I want. Tranquil maybe. Or calming."

"Glad you like it here. I hope you'll come back often, Olivia."

"You really mean that, Forrest?" she asks, taken off guard by the sincerity in his voice.

"I do. I would miss our little meetings."

Emboldened as she has never been before with Forrest, Olivia figures if there is ever to be an appropriate time to reveal her feelings, this is it. She plunges ahead before her nerve fails her.

"Forrest, I may never get another setting like this to tell you something I've wanted to say for a long time. We're all alone. Nobody even within shouting distance. No phones. No business to distract us. So here goes.

"I've been trying in vain to send little hints and signals that I'd like more than a friendship with you. In the three years I've been our firm's main attorney assigned to you, I've discovered you to be honest, intelligent, extraordinarily considerate and patient, and just a generally good man."

Blushing slightly, Olivia looks straight into his hazel eyes and opens her heart. "You're also handsome, athletically fit, beautifully dressed, and you have a good sense of humor."

"You forgot sexy, desirable, and irresistible," Forrest exaggerates, trying to put both of them more at ease.

"Seriously, Olivia, I've gotten the signals, and believe me, I've wanted many times to act on them. But you know my story now that I've told you about the mansion and Maggie and all that. The truth is I'm genuinely scared to get involved again in a serious romance.

"I mean, you see yourself in the mirror every day; you know you're great looking. Any man would find you desirable, but I'm not just any other man. I am as attracted by your intelligence as your looks. To me, intelligence is sexy. And you are super bright. You're also charming, articulate, and you can blend in and hold your own in any situation. You've got everything."

"Then why not give me a try, Forrest?"

"Because, I repeat, I am literally afraid. And I don't think you have considered how I would work out in a relationship. I've been a loner for more than twenty years, and I cherish having my space. I'm not used to having someone around me for long periods of time. I'm accustomed to coming and going as I please and answering to no one—except for the demands of business."

"I'm not asking you to marry me, Forrest. Just to spend some time with me in a variety of settings and see what, if anything, happens. Would you be willing to at least try that for a little while?"

"Tell you what, Olivia. You said you could stay until Monday, so I have a suggestion, and if it suits you, it will give us a chance to spend some time together. It also will give me an opportunity to introduce you to a little more of southern West Virginia. I think it's important for you to find out what life and the people are like here because this is my home.

Somewhere in between, we'll work in the investigators' report you came here to deliver."

"My pretext," she admits.

"Whatever," Forrest dismisses with a boyish grin. "Anyway, I've been intending to drive to a little town called Bramwell in Mercer County to get some ideas for the mansion. We could stop on the way at Grandview State Park in Raleigh County. There's an overlook there where you can see miles down to a river with railroad tracks running beside it and the remains of an old mining town—we call them coal camps. I guarantee you'll see how high up we are after looking over the edge of the park because as many times as I've experienced that dizzying view, I still grip the top of the rail and lean backward.

"Then when we get to Mercer County, which borders Raleigh, we can have lunch at Pipestem State Park. I remember how good the food was in the dining room, and it has a really good view, too."

"I'd love that, Forrest. But I'm curious to know about Bramwell. What does that 'little town' have that would give you ideas for your place?"

"Well, listen to this. Little Bramwell has been known as the 'home of the millionaires' since it was incorporated near the end of the nineteenth century. More than a dozen coal barons and wealthy businessmen built mansions there at one time, and a good number of the houses are still standing.

"If my memory is accurate, one house had an indoor pool, another a ballroom on its third floor, and one a roof made out of copper and slate. All of them, I think, had ornate woodwork, high ceilings, and stained-glass windows. At one time, Bramwell had more millionaires per capita than any other place in the country. True story.

"I think you'll enjoy just walking around and looking at them."

Chapter Seven

Tall Mountains and Coal Baron Mansions

They leave early the next morning, taking Olivia's rented Mustang because it's new and has air conditioning, unlike Forrest's old Chevy sedan. They spent the night in Forrest's cabin—but not together. He insisted she stay in its one bedroom while he bunked on the large sofa.

After breakfast at a Cracker Barrel restaurant—where Forrest insisted Olivia sample flour-based sawmill gravy on her biscuits, along with salty country ham—they make their way on the backroads to Grandview State Park, about a forty-five-minute drive.

"Unless a person is in a hurry, it's always best to skip the interstates," Forrest explains. "You can see some pretty scenery from I-64 and I-77, but you miss the little towns and the two-lane roads with miles of countryside and the farm animals. I mean, how often do you see cows and horses on your way to work, Olivia?"

She touches Forrest's shoulder and laughs. "About as often as you see skyscrapers among these red barns. But I'm glad you brought me this way. I'm really enjoying myself."

When they are within ten miles of the park, Forrest heads the car up the hills until he reaches an elevation of three thousand feet. But Olivia still has no sense of being on top of a mountain. "Won't be long, Olivia. You'll get all the height you want at the overlook."

"When I was growing up, Grandview had none of these big expensive houses," Forrest says, pointing out the widely scattered homes with acres of property surrounding most of them. "All I saw were some modest wooden houses and a store or two. But with the interstate highways making access so much easier, people with money are taking advantage of a beautiful place to live."

As they round a curve, the park comes into view. They leave their car in the parking lot and walk up the rock path toward the rim, passing by the Cliffside Amphitheatre, which takes Olivia by surprise. "Why didn't you tell me there was an outdoor theater here," she says with genuine interest.

"Oh, just another of those things I take for granted but shouldn't," Forrest answers. "During the summer months, a historical drama is performed about the Hatfields and the McCoys, the infamous feuding families. You've heard about them, haven't you?"

"I know there was a big feud but little else."

"Well, Olivia, the Hatfields were from southwestern West Virginia and the McCoys from neighboring Kentucky. That's why that particular drama is held here year after year. They also do other shows from time to time, and if you visit during the summer, I'll take you, if you'd like."

"I would absolutely love it, Forrest. Promise?"

"I promise. Now, let's go look miles and miles over a mountain."

***

"Wow! Oh, wow! You weren't exaggerating, Forrest. Dear God, I feel as if I'm looking out of an airplane window. What is that river way down there winding between all those rows of mountains?"

"That's the oddly misnamed New River, running through the New River Gorge National Park. There used to be some coal towns and railroad tracks down there, too."

"It is breathtaking, Forrest. But scary. I understand why you said you always hang onto the railing. I'm gripping it so tightly my hands hurt. But you didn't say why the New River is misnamed."

"That's kind of a surprise to everybody, Olivia. You see, the New River is millions of years old—among the three oldest rivers in the world, I'm told. It is the oldest river in North America, and, oddly enough, it runs north. It's beautiful, but it can be dangerous with strong undercurrents and rapids. Rafting companies do a big tourist business with thousands of people adventurous enough to take the challenge."

"Good luck to them, Forrest. I'll go to the amphitheater with you and hike some of the park trails, but this old city gal ain't gonna get anywhere near rapids!"

Forrest returns her grin without admitting that although he has relatives and friends who have rafted many times, he himself has not. And he is not at all sure he would.

"You about ready to eat again, now that you've braved the dizzying heights of West Virginia? We're less than an hour's drive from Pipestem State Park."

"Ready and willing," she says, wrapping her right arm around Forrest's waist and kissing him lightly on his left cheek, hoping for a reaction. All she gets in return is a pat of his left hand on her shoulder and another smile.

"Well, that's something, I guess," she says to herself, still determined to keep testing this man she finds more and more attractive and challenging.

"We'll skip the interstate again and drive down by the Bluestone Dam near Hinton in Summers County. It's a pretty way to go, and I want to stop at the Dairy Queen and buy you one of the best hot dogs you'll ever eat. But you have to eat it West Virginia style."

"And what's that, Forrest? Is it made out of bear meat or possum or something equally exotic?"

"No, nothing like that," he chuckles, appreciating her being such a good sport. "It comes loaded with mustard, onions, chili, and cole slaw.

And absolutely no sauerkraut, or relish. Not while you're with me. And we'll have just one each, so we don't spoil our appetites for the food at Pipestem."

"Are we going to eat in the car, or is there a restaurant area?"

"Not only is there a seating area, Olivia, but part of the restaurant extends out over the river. That's where we're going to sit. You'll love it. Everybody does."

***

Underway again, they pass by the massive Bluestone Dam where a number of fishermen have gathered on the banks. Olivia, who has never been fishing in her life, is surprised to see a bunch of men, and a few women, using more than one pole apiece. They each have two or three anchored to the ground and are holding another in their hands.

"Do you know what's going on with those people?" she asks Forrest.

"What do you mean? I don't see anything unusual."

"I don't understand why they have poles that look like they are stuck in the ground. How can they fish with more than one pole at a time?"

Forrest smiles again. There's so much about home he takes for granted that he has to continually remind himself a city girl knows little or nothing about. "They're trying to catch different kinds of fish, Olivia. They're probably fishing for bass, crappie or bluegill with the pole they are carrying. The anchored poles are for carp and catfish. I've heard they can be three feet long and weigh sixty or seventy pounds, especially near the base of the dam."

"Can you eat all those kinds of fish?"

"You can, but I wouldn't. Most people won't eat carp; they just catch them for fun and release them. Bass, crappie, bluegill, and some catfish are good to eat."

"Do you fish or hunt, Forrest?"

"I did a little fishing when I was a boy, but I've never been hunting. I have many friends and relatives who do both. But I'm like my mother, I guess, because she said she liked to think meat originated in the supermarket."

"All this talk about food is making me hungry, Forrest. What's on our lunch menu?"

"That depends on whether we eat in the main restaurant or take the tram a couple of thousand feet down the mountain and eat in the restaurant at the bottom. I don't know whether the food is different in each place, but we can check."

"Oh, I definitely want to take the tram. Can we do that, Forrest?" she asks excitedly.

"Sure. Whatever you want."

***

When the big stone entrance comes into view, Forrest turns off Pipestem Drive and goes three miles through country scenery to the main lodge. Looking around, he sees a sign that points the way to the tram.

Forrest need not have worried about Olivia's being afraid of the ride down the steep mountain. She loves the scenery and the warm breeze, although she is slightly disappointed at not seeing a bear or a wolf or a moose.

Forrest grins again. "We do have black bears, Olivia, but they shy away from people most of the time. On the other hand, wolves have been reintroduced into some parts of the state, but seeing one is rare. As far as moose are concerned, you're in the wrong part of the country. We have hundreds of thousands of deer, but no moose, I'm sorry to have to tell you."

After they are seated in the restaurant by a window with a grand view, Forrest looks at the menu and smiles. "They've got it, Olivia. We're going to have country steak and gravy, mashed potatoes, green beans, creamed corn, cloverleaf yeast rolls, iced tea, and blackberry cobbler with ice cream. Before ordering, he asks the server to bring a small piece of the steak, which he cuts not with a knife but with the edge of his fork. He nods his approval.

Intrigued and puzzled, Olivia asks, "What was that all about, Forrest?"

"That, my friend, was the Forrest Alderson Country Steak Test. If it's prepared right, the steak goes into a pressure cooker to make it super tender and then it's fried in a skillet to give it a nice crust. But, and this is the real test, it's only fit to eat if you can cut it with the dull edge of a fork. If you have to use a knife, it's too tough, and I wouldn't order it."

When the food arrives, Forrest enjoys it so much he hardly says a word until dessert is served. "Well, Olivia, what do you think? Really, I mean."

Fortunately, she liked it almost as much as Forrest did. If she hadn't, she'd already determined to fib to keep from spoiling an experience he so wanted her to enjoy.

"Fabulous, Forrest. I even liked the gravy."

Forrest beams, pulls her chair out for her and places his arm loosely around her waist as they leave the building.

"Well I'll be damned," she thinks. "Dare I feel encouraged?"

***

The drive from Pipestem to Bramwell takes less than an hour. It is located just above Bluefield, the largest city in Mercer County, which borders the state of Virginia.

"Charming, Forrest. It looks like a picture postcard. Can we just park and walk around or do we need to drive from one place to another?"

"Let's walk. It's such a pretty day, and everything we want to see is within easy distance for a couple of people who need to work off a heavy meal. Let's start with the old Presbyterian church. I think it's open to visitors, and you'll want to see the native bluestone it's made of. Should be some people there to ask if tours of the town are still available, although that's unlikely because I seem to recall people open their houses to the public only a couple of times a year."

They enter the church and sit reverently in one of the comfortable pews. The church is not large, but it is impressive. Forrest and Olivia learn from the available literature that the church was built in 1904 by Italian stonemasons who cut and laid the local bluestone.

"Those Italians were true artisans, Olivia. They worked all over the coal fields in southern West Virginia, and a lot of what they constructed is so sturdy it's still standing, including some old company stores and retaining walls they built where roads run up against the sides of hills."

"Well, I'm impressed, Forrest. It's as good as any stonework I've seen in Chicago."

"Ready to go look at some big, magnificent houses?"

"Absolutely! Lead on, native son."

If Forrest erred in his earlier descriptions of what to expect in Bramwell, it was on the side of understatement, as far as Olivia is concerned. Even though the grand houses are not open, visitors can walk right up to the property line to take in the Cooper House with its turret, curved porch, copper roof, and orange brick; the English Tudor Thomas house that overlooks the town and features a ballroom; the Victorian Era Goodwill House that stands above the Bluestone River and also has a ballroom and a tower; and quite a few others.

"Sorry, it's getting dark, Olivia. I know you would like to stay longer, but we'd better get back to the cabin. I'm going to see if I can get someone with local influence to set up a private tour for a fee or a donation to the town or whatever. I've gotten some ideas from walking around today, but I'm eager to see how these homes look inside. My mansion was built about the same time as these, so I should see something I can use for a model."

Not letting a potential opportunity slip away, Olivia quickly says, "I always have vacation time accrued, Forrest, and I'll never forgive you if you don't invite me." She drives the point home with a pretty smile and a couple of fist taps on his shoulder.

Chapter Eight

Forrest's Romantic Fears

"Get a nice fire going, Forrest, and I'll fix us a snack and a drink. Ham and cheese sandwiches and some chardonnay OK with you?"

"Sounds great. I'll get some wood."

Forrest finishes his chore at about the same time as Olivia steps from the kitchen with two trays of food, looking for a place to set them. Forrest suggests they sit near the fire, and Olivia's quick mind figures moving the sofa instead of two chairs would be "cozier."

"Fun day, Forrest," Olivia says between bites of her sandwich.

"Glad you had a good time," he smiles. "I did, too. You're not such bad company after all," he teases.

"Think you could put up with me again?" she counters.

"I'll say yes if you'll keep my glass filled. It's my favorite wine."

Olivia does as he asks, then collects the trays and takes them to the kitchen, and after tidying up the sofa, she grabs a quilt, sits beside Forrest so closely they are touching, and places the cover over both of them.

"Do me another favor?" she asks, turning her head so she is just inches from his face.

"Sure. What?"

"Don't mention my work until I leave Monday morning to catch the flight to Chicago. I am so content and happy right now, I don't want to spoil my mood thinking about what's facing me at the office."

"No problem for me," Forrest says, surprising Olivia by moving his right arm behind her neck and over her right shoulder. She snuggles closer and leans her head onto his chest and neck. They sit quietly for a while, neither moving, just enjoying being together, pleasantly shut off from the rest of the world, alone in front of burning logs that smell a little like maple syrup.

They lift their heads spontaneously, and with a look that gives each other permission to shed their incertitude, they kiss. It isn't a peck between friends, or a brushing of lips as a couple might do in a greeting. It is a hot, full-on-the-lips tasting between two people releasing pent-up desire. But it is short-lasting.

Both are a little shocked and embarrassed. What happened on the spur-of-the-moment, just happened. There was no planning, no maneuvering, nothing forced or awkward. If anything, it was about as innocent as it could be.

"Did that scare you, Forrest?" Olivia asks jokingly, but she seriously wants to know.

"I don't know yet, but if it didn't, it should. It's been a long, long time . . . decades, really, since I've had an authentically romantic kiss. If you were any other woman, Olivia, I think I'd be running away by now."

"Want to try it again?" Olivia offers, lifting her mouth eagerly to join with Forrest's. This time, they wrap their arms around each other and kiss passionately. But when Forrest feels the tip of Olivia's tongue divide his lips, he trembles and pulls back.

As a forty-year-old woman who has been married and pursued by many men, Olivia is romantically and sexually experienced, but never has she had a man withdraw as Forrest has. But even in a passionate moment, Olivia's intelligence and insightfulness serve her well. Forrest's trembling is not triggered by passion but by genuine fear. Olivia realizes she has unintentionally moved deeper and faster into a relationship than Forrest is psychologically prepared to handle.

"I'm sorry," he apologizes, quite embarrassed.

"It's OK, really," she reassures him. "But let's talk, Forrest. I know how deeply you've been hurt, and that it's going to take whatever time it takes for you to overcome that. I'm patient and I am understanding. Please know that."

"Thanks, Olivia. It's good of you not to berate me and pack up and go. I want to kiss you, to hold you, to make love to you. But I'm scared. I don't think I can survive another breakup romantic love can cause. I just can't go through that again."

"I think I understand, Forrest. But tell me, if you are willing, what you have done for love and sex all these years. I'd hate to think you went through your twenties, thirties, and early forties completely celibate."

"I'll answer candidly if you will give me your word that what I say remains between you and me. I trust you as I trust few, if any, other people, so if you promise, I'll tell you."

"I have many flaws, Forrest, but I am honest and can be trusted. I give you my word."

"Then I hope you will not be shocked to hear I've had sex countless times with a great many women since I left West Virginia. But never romantic sex, and never within five hundred miles of Chicago. Rich men have no problem buying sex from high-class, well-educated, healthy, sophisticated courtesans.

"So, what scares me with a wonderful, intelligent, loving woman like you? It's the romance. The commitment. The fear of falling hopelessly in love with you and then losing you.

"Those other women meant nothing to me other than the fact that they were human beings that I treated well and wished only well for them. But sex for the simple pleasure of it is worlds different from romantic sex. When it's over, I can't wait for the women to walk out the door and out of my life forever. When the passion has cooled, I always find it hard to believe I even wanted any of them so badly.

"But with romantic love, the kind I truly had with Maggie, it's not like animal rutting. In romantic sex, the man is more concerned for his woman's satisfaction than for his own, and when it's over, he still wants to be with her. If they are not married, and she has to return to her own home, he counts the minutes until he can be with her again. No one, not even his parents and his siblings—no matter how much he loves them— are as important to him as she is.

"That's the kind of love I'm scared of, Olivia. And that's the kind of love I would have with you if I allowed myself to, and you loved me back.

"Now do you understand me?"

"I do, Forrest. If I were an inexperienced young woman, I would not. But I've been through enough romantic joy and heartbreak to understand. And as I told you before, I am patient. I will not hurt you.

"Forrest, look directly at me and listen carefully to my words: *I am not Maggie.* You can rely on that. I promise.

"Now, hold me and let's just enjoy the fire and the rest of this special day you've given me."

Chapter Nine

Who's Who and Who's Where

After spending a second night sleeping separately, Forrest and Olivia take a leisurely walk in the woods, followed by a breakfast of pancakes, scrambled eggs, and coffee. Then it's down to the business of discussing the report Olivia could have delivered over the telephone but used as an excuse for her visit.

"I know how you hate to have things dragged out, Forrest, so I'll get directly to it. I received a comprehensive report on everything from the team of investigators we put together a few weeks ago, and I boiled it down to the essentials for you. Do you want me to hit the highlights and let you read the details for yourself?"

"Yes, Olivia. Let's hear it."

"OK, first, Maggie's still living in Asher Heights, but I'll come to her later. Roughly a third of the three hundred fourteen members of your Class of 1959 are still in the area including three you played basketball with on Whitney Rutherford's backyard court. Whitney is not among them though, and his family no longer owns the property beside the mansion. But Whitney's not far away. He and his brothers inherited their father's construction company and moved its headquarters to Charleston.

"Chris Mathis, Sandy Overmeyer, and Stretch Maddox live in the suburbs, but judging from their recent photos, Chris and Sandy are carrying too much weight for basketball anymore, and although Stretch is still tall and skinny, he has arthritic knees after playing basketball for more than twenty years from junior high to the pros leagues in Europe."

"Glad to hear they're still around," Forrest says. "What kind of businesses are they in?"

"Well, you can buy either a Cadillac or an Oldsmobile from Stretch. He bought both agencies with the money he made as a pro. Chris runs a furniture company, and Sandy is office manager for Appalachian Power Company. They're all married and have kids. Good, solid citizens, as far as we know.

"Moving on, the bad news is seventeen of your classmates have died —none of whom you checked off in your yearbook as being among your circle of friends. I'll give you a list of them, but a special one I should tell you about is Art Daniels, who died in Vietnam and was awarded the Silver Star."

"My goodness," Forrest says softly. "I didn't know Art well because he was a bus student who just came to school and went home. He didn't play sports or anything, but he was a good student and a good guy. I hate to hear he's dead, but I'm proud to know he died a hero."

"The three teachers you wanted to know about are all retired. Mr. Scott and Mrs. Blankenship moved with their spouses to Florida, but Coach Hendrickson still lives in the same house he and his wife bought a zillion years ago. I know you'll want to contact him when you think the time is right to 'reveal' yourself.

"And, by the way," Olivia grins with three quick wiggles of her expertly waxed eyebrows, "a few of your old flames are still around, too. Remember Betty Sue Earl, Caroline Baker, and Misty Springer? Betty Sue is married with two teenagers, but the other two are available, if you're interested. Caroline is divorced with three children and Misty has never married. The pictures our investigators took of Caroline indicate she still looks pretty darn good; Misty, on the other hand, has porked up quite a bit."

"Just move along with your report," Forrest deadpans with no hint of interest in his heartthrobs of long ago.

"Gee, I was hoping to see a teeny sparkle in your eyes, Forrest. You're not going to let me have any fun with this report, are you? Rats!

"You may already have learned your old high school was torn down and students from Clinton High and Alexander High have all been consolidated into Asher Heights High School, which looks like a small college campus. Oh, and the 'junior high' is now a 'middle school' for grades six through eight. No more seventh through ninth grade junior highs. Ninth graders are now part of the high school."

"Olivia, I have driven for hours through the town and the county, so I've seen the businesses that have moved to the malls or near the interstate exchanges. And I've taken notice of missing buildings and the ones that have taken their place. I've also been back to all my old hangouts—or at least those still in existence. I think I know enough from you to let the written report speak for itself. I'll get back to you if I have follow-up requests for the investigators.

"Now, tell me about Maggie. Every little detail we've found out."

Olivia takes a deep breath and begins. But her fact-filled report cannot possibly explain the woman Maggie's life experiences have turned her into. Perhaps even Maggie is not fully aware herself.

Chapter Ten

Maggie Maneuvers a Comeback

Like an agile alley cat, Maggie McDaniel Mullens landed nimbly on her feet after falling out of grace over a disastrous marriage to bad boy LeRoy Bottoms, whose only contributions to their brief union were her nightmare of memories and his unintentional service as a sperm donor.

Three years after a ten-month marriage to that habitual absentee, Maggie manuevered herself into luxury by bride-stepping down the aisle into a mutually beneficial arrangement with Broderick Nathaniel Buckingham IV, an intelligent, well-educated but hopelessly nerdy son of one of the most prominent and wealthy families in the state.

Both Maggie and "Nat" were soberly aware of the unspoken but clear implications of their legal bonding. She wanted restoration of her reputation, a stable home for her daughter, and a lavish lifestyle. Despite his family's strong objections to his choice for a bride, he wanted something his unfortunate physical unattractiveness, his social awkwardness, and his malignantly boring personality had robbed him of all his life: an intelligent, socially graceful, sexy trophy woman whose circumstances were so dire she would be his accommodating bedmate and social companion in return for all the benefits of the Buckingham name.

Maggie did not love him, and he knew it. Neither had illusions about what their lives together would be like. She expected him to be kind and generous, to be a good father to her daughter, and to treat her with respect both in private and in public. He expected her to fulfill his sexual desires, to be his entrée into the in-crowd that would surely embrace her, to be faithful, and to conduct herself respectably.

Nat had suffered terribly from romantic and sexual rejection since junior high school. He also was resigned to the fact he could never have been Maggie's first husband, no matter what his family had to offer. Cinderella, he knew all too well, would not settle for someone like him when she could have the man she perceived to be her Prince Charming.

But a boring, unattractive man who was also rich and from an upper-crust family might appeal to a woman who had already paid dearly for a few intoxicatingly passionate months with a storybook man her misguided notions of love and sex had tricked her into thinking LeRoy represented. Those illusions disappeared soon after her pregnancy began reshaping her body, and her turned-off lover resumed stalking less encumbered beauties.

Nat had often questioned why God grants handsome faces and desirable bodies to the LeRoy Bottomses of the world while handicapping decent males like him and countless other plain, lonely men and women. The answer, he concluded long ago, defies understanding.

Beautiful women and handsome men begin life with advantages; extraordinarily beautiful women and extraordinarily handsome men begin with extraordinary advantages – a universal truth Maggie and LeRoy know only too well and exploit for all it's worth.

***

Marrying Nat Buckingham boosted Maggie over the most crucial hurdle in her scheme to seize for herself the secure future that that mirage of a man LeRoy Bottoms had hoodwinked her out of. But marriage to a wealthy man from a prominent family was just Step One.

Maggie put Step Two into effect on her wedding night. The sexually deprived Nat had not the vaguest clue his tantalizingly seductive wife was about to circumvent the prenuptial agreement designed to leave her with only a hundred thousand dollars should she have an affair or divorce him. Her weapon? A conniving woman's knowledge that under the heat of passion, a man will say or do almost anything for that other thing.

By fulfilling every sexual daydream Nat had ever imagined, Maggie acquired her cancel proof "insurance policy" within a year. Nat's son arrived a month sooner than his first wedding anniversary. The child, as Maggie had intended, guaranteed her a generous money pipeline to the Buckinghams even if she one day decided she couldn't bear living any longer with a man whose physical attentions made her skin crawl.

Meanwhile, the confidentiality constraints between physician and patient kept her husband from knowing *The Fix* was in. A tubal ligation ensured she would have no more children, and her chronic "female problems," self-diagnosed following the birth of Broderick Nathaniel Buckingham V, gave Maggie a plausible excuse for dodging Nat's sexual advances.

Devious, deceitful Maggie had outmaneuvered Nat so deftly, he didn't realize he'd been exiled from her bedroom until after the door was virtually locked.

***

A lifestyle that only the Buckingham name and money can give her persuades Maggie to stay in the marriage, so she and Nat are still living under the same roof eighteen years later when Forrest moves back to Asher Heights. She grants Nat entry into her bedroom just often enough to keep him from divorcing her. She is smart enough to restrict her extra-marital escapades to distant vacation spots she visits frequently, certain that Nat does likewise.

Chapter Eleven

Mansion Triggers Maggie's Jealousy

Living in one of the finest houses in Asher Heights isn't nearly enough to keep Maggie Buckingham from stewing in envy when she hears the Malcolmsons have sold Old Mrs. Kimble's mansion and moved to Mountaineer Manor. Had it occurred to her that Louisa and Alistair would consider leaving the place permanently while still alive, she would have made Nat's life a living hell until he cried uncle, buying the place to gain a year or two of peaceful benign neglect while Maggie gleefully busied herself restoring and refurnishing it to her heart's content.

"Could have been the Queen Bee of the county sitting on the throne in that house," she fantasizes, knowing only too well the meteoritic rise in prestige and status that fully restored mansion would instantly bestow on her. "Hope the damn woman who gets to live there is old, saggy, wrinkled, and uglier than homemade sin," she swears. "If I had any faith in voodoo, I'd go out right now and get me a doll and a very long, sharp pin.

"Nat, I want to know who bought the mansion, how much they paid, and what they intend to do with it. You know everybody; you can find out by noon today if you try."

"I've already anticipated you, my dear," Nat monotones in reply. "The buyer paid two million dollars for it, didn't use his name on the deed, and I have no clue who he is or what his plans are. I can tell you the house is terribly run-down and will cost a fortune to restore. Whoever bought it apparently has more money than he has good sense. It's a bottomless money hole of an investment."

"Can't your family pull some strings and uncover his identity?"

"Don't think so, Maggie."

Not one to give up easily, Maggie pauses thoughtfully for a minute, then demands Nat hire a team of investigators to spy on the place twenty-four hours a day.

"The buyer has to have a contractor, and the contractor has to have roofers, painters, construction workers, appliance installers, and all that. Oh, and I'm going to invite those lawyers, John Vermillion and Cassandra What's-Her-Name, to dinner next Saturday night, ply them with the best whiskey we can buy, and pump the hell out of them until they let a tidbit or two slip out."

"If you say so, dear," Nat concedes, knowing from long experience the futility of begging off.

"I'm going to make some phone calls, Nat. Somebody in this town knows something, and I'm going to find out what it is."

"Good idea," Nat encourages, figuring Maggie will talk the rest of the morning away. And, thankfully, not with him.

Chapter Twelve

A Bizarre Discovery

Forrest was prepared for unanticipated problems during the mansion's renovation stage. Complications are the rule instead of the exception in a huge house nearly one hundred years old and deteriorating from decades of neglect. But nobody could have seen this one coming.

"Hope you have a stiff drink handy, Forrest," Olivia warns in a three thirty p.m. telephone call soon after repairs begin.

"Uh-oh, Olivia. I hate suspense. What is it?"

"Workers discovered a small secret room in the attic while they were tearing out the collapsed ceiling and two walls in a bedroom. You wouldn't guess in a million years what they found."

"I repeat: I hate suspense, Olivia. And I'm not going to guess. Let's have it."

"They found a shrine, Forrest. An honest-to-God authentic shrine with framed pictures of Old Mrs. Kimble and her young husband, a family Bible, a full-sized statue of the Virgin Mary, candelabra, an altar, and one comfortable chair. And, get this, one large bronze urn containing the couple's mixed ashes. Can you believe that?!"

"Well, shit fire and save the matches!"

Forrest's paternal grandfather's favorite exclamation rolls spontaneously off his tongue. "That is bizarre. But how do you know the urn contains both of their remains?"

"Mrs. Kimble left a note explaining everything. She had this secret room built so she could 'spend time with her husband' over the years and had an unidentified relative mix their ashes and seal the room after she died.

"The note makes a request, too, which takes care of what you can do with the room and its contents if you and her remaining family—that would be Louisa and Alistair—are willing. She wants the room left as is and sealed back up. Honestly, that's what she requested."

"Well, what do you think, Olivia?"

"Sounds simultaneously very loving and eternally romantic but also creepy to me. The big question is can you live with that in your house?"

"OK, I'll have John Vermillion contact the Malcolmsons and get their input. If they insist on moving the urn to a mausoleum, or, highly unlikely, keeping it at their condo, that's what I'll do. If they want to leave it as is in the house, I suppose I can do that.

"No way to keep this a secret now that the construction crew knows about it. Couldn't expect them not to talk about it. Probably shocked the absolute hell out of them when they discovered it. Besides, it will only add to the mystique of the mansion itself. You know, Old Mrs. Kimble living there as a recluse for decades and all."

"Good, Forrest. I mean 'good' because it's your problem now. I'd like to say for you to call on me if I can be of further help in this matter, but I'd prefer to get this out of my mind if I can. As I said before, I find Old Mrs. Kimble's devotion to her husband's memory very touching. But that room gives me the heebie-jeebies. And, Forrest, if you ever invite me to spend the night in your mansion, I won't be making any trips to the attic."

Chapter Thirteen

Forrest Completes Plans for the Mansion

Three months after making his dream purchase, Forrest meets Olivia in her Chicago law office, along with an architect, a civil engineer, and two interior decorators representing firms he has hired to oversee the restoration and the decorating of his mansion. He is eager to hear their recommendations and move full-speed ahead.

Forrest previously had made clear to each of them he was going to follow his own tastes and judgment, but he welcomed their input and suggestions on everything related to the restoration and furnishing.

"I want the main and upper floors to be accurate to the time in which the house was built. But I am neither a stickler nor a conformist in every detail. If you cannot locate all the furniture and fixtures from that time period, reproductions will suit me just fine.

"As far as paintings, sculptures and things of that sort are concerned, I am not a collector. Extremely well-done reproductions will do just fine. I'm willing to spend any amount of money necessary to complete my house, but I'm just not interested in shelling out millions for an original Van Gogh, Monet, or Rembrandt."

Forrest has been paying particular attention to the expressions on the faces of his experts, gauging how receptive and, perhaps, enthusiastic they appear. "So far, so good," he believes. "But there's no way in hell they're prepared for what I'm going to hit them with before they leave."

Because Forrest has allowed too long a pause during his assessment, the architect speaks up. "Do you have specific plans for the basement and attic, Forrest? Or are you going to use them primarily for storage?"

"I'm going to have some fun with the basement," Forrest beams, devilishly eager to disclose his plans but wanting to get the business part of the meeting out of the way first.

"We'll come to that later. First, let me remind you that in all we do, I want to use West Virginia artisans and other workers, as well as all the materials I can get from local businesses. Each of you has, or will soon have, a local counterpart from Asher Heights or nearby with whom you will coordinate and carry out your plans.

"The first thing on the agenda today is to determine the integrity and soundness of the structure itself. Alejandro Cruz of The L.T. Lodge Corporation will give us his report."

"Thank you, Forrest. The news is mixed. For a structure almost one hundred years old, the foundation and the walls are in generally good condition, especially considering no significant maintenance has been done in a long period. The roof, however, will need to be totally replaced, and internal reinforcement is recommended throughout the house to ensure the building will remain sound for decades. That will be expensive."

The architect, Margaret Tutwiler of Tutwiler, Novak, and Manchester, presents sketches and blueprints for the construction of a guest apartment over the existing four-car garage, and for internal changes Forrest has requested for removing walls to enlarge rooms on all floors. Tutwiler also presents plans for several unusual requests Forrest has made.

The interior decorators, Christina Merryweather and Patrick O'Donnell of Majestic Interior Designs, have presentations for the late nineteenth century furnishings Forrest wants for the first and second floors.

Forrest himself has only three rooms he wants total design control over. To her great delight, he has given Olivia permission to supervise the rest of the house, subject only to his final approval.

On the recommendation of trusted friends, Forrest chose Christina and Patrick because he was assured they not only were thoroughly knowledgeable and professional but also flamboyant and adventurous. They won him over when they laughed at his description of his tastes as "stopping one step short of gaudy."

Forrest's surprise: He wants to recreate one of his fondest memories, so he is having the basement converted to a fifties soda shop/diner, complete with a black and white tile dance floor, a Wurlitzer *One More Time* Jukebox, a long red counter with spinner-top stools, and lots and lots of chrome and red Formica.

"And I want to cover the walls in metal signs of fifties cars, movie posters, and pictures of popular singers and other celebrities. And everywhere I look, I want to see neon lights glowing."

The surprised looks on the faces of Olivia and the interior decorators prompt Forrest to add, "I know some purists would consider a room like that in a dignified old mansion to be a desecration. But I don't care. It's my house and my money and what I want."

"That plan comes as quite a shock to me and, I presume, to my associates as well," Margaret Tutwiler admits with amusement. "But as I think about it, the more I love the idea. Forrest and I are about the same age, so I share his nostalgia about that time period. We should have no trouble providing the open space needed without weakening the support necessary for the rest of the house. And, Forrest, if I dig around in my attic, I'm confident I'll find a bunch of old 45RPM records to donate for your jukebox."

His mother also has made a very sensible request Forrest had not considered. She reminded him that, although he is still quite fit, he will inevitably age, and so will his family and friends. "You need an elevator, Forrest," Virginia Alderson advised. "I'm not prepared to run up and down steep flights of stairs whenever I visit, and your older friends aren't either. You also need a master bedroom and a full bathroom on the first floor for the same reasons."

Forrest orders it done, but the architects tell him they must build the elevator as an attachment to the back of the house and construct entrances for each floor. That will require an adjustment for the other built-on room Forrest originally wanted to center on the back wall. For both projects, he already knows he wants to use the same native bluestone he saw on the old Presbyterian church in Bramwell.

The most personally important room is his library, which he plans to the finest detail, expecting it to be by far his favorite of all the magnificent rooms in the grand mansion. It is to be his inner sanctum, his safe place, his escape from reality, his buffer between himself and all of life's demands, pressures, threats, and invasions of privacy. A select number of others may be invited to spend time with him in it, but none will share it. It will be his exclusive space.

When he sits at his massive, ornately-carved Rosewood desk or rests in his favorite leather chair, or reclines on his overstuffed couch, he will be surrounded by a room he personally designed and filled with objects painstakingly chosen for the feelings they evoke of peace, privacy, protection, and beauty.

The high-ceiling room will be lit not only by electricity but also by sunlight beaming in through two three-panel bay windows featuring seven-foot-sized stained-glass depictions of his favorite American authors. Mark Twain, O. Henry, and Frank Yerby will occupy the left bay panels and Willa Cather, Louis L'Amour, and Edna Ferber those on the right.

The American chestnut floors will be complemented by maple walls and bookshelves and strategically placed paintings of Forrest's favorite West Virginia scenery. He has commissioned paintings of Blackwater Falls, the main overlook at Grandview State Park, the state capitol from the far side of the Kanawha River, and the view overlooking the historic town of Harpers Ferry, among others. Forrest wants four paintings completed of each so he can interchange them to match the seasons.

For reasons he himself does not fully understand, Forrest feels a need for a semicircular addition to the back of the house. He will call it his "meditation" room, but it also could be an unconventionally shaped chapel. Part of his motivation is his love of stained glass, not being satisfied with having it limited to his library.

The bottom four feet of the forty-five-foot interior curved wall will be made of black walnut wood. The upper portion will consist of fifteen panels of glass, each eight-feet high and three-feet wide. The first panel on each side will connect with the house, and the three in the center will be plain beveled glass to allow as much natural light as possible to penetrate into the room. The centermost panel will have a chrystal cross covering almost its entire length and width.

The remaining ten panels will be stained-glass depictions of inspirational events from the Bible. Forrest already knows he wants to commission a panel featuring John baptizing Jesus, another of Paul's conversion on the road to Damascus, a third of Jesus raising Lazarus from the dead, and a fourth of Michelangelo's Pieta, the sculpture of Mary holding the body of Jesus on her lap and in her arms. For the other six, he will seek guidance from ministers representing a variety of churches.

Forrest's good mother made certain her family went to church as a group every Sunday they could possibly attend, as well as on special holidays. At home they prayed as a group before Sunday, Thanksgiving, Christmas, and Easter dinners. Forrest is a lifelong believer, but as an adult, he attended church only sparingly. He always had better intentions, and he hopes a meditation room/chapel will help him follow his mother's wishes for him more faithfully.

***

After the others leave, Forrest says to Olivia, "You were uncharacteristically quiet during the meeting. I have a feeling you were saving something just for me. Have I read you accurately?"

"You have indeed. I've been so excited with all the freedom you've given me over the furnishing and decorating, I've come up with an idea for the attic I hope you're going to love."

Refreshing his coffee and picking up another chocolate doughnut, Forrest takes a seat opposite Olivia and lifts his hands palm-upward signaling he's ready to hear her out.

"In the trips I've made to Asher Heights, I've learned how much pride you take in your state and in its people, their talents, and their way of life in general. You've taken me to a number of arts and crafts festivals, country music events, the state fair, and some other places that display their artistic talents, and I have been sincerely impressed. So, here's my proposal. And, by the way, you've made this easier by already going against tradition with that fifties basement.

"Forrest, I think we should furnish the entire attic with Appalachian arts and crafts, using old barnwood for the floors and walls, handmade furniture, light fixtures, paintings, pottery, quilts—everything! How does that strike you?"

"Well, first it tells me we just might make a pretty fair hillbilly out of you after all. Second, it lets me know that smart mind of yours has been working overtime. You really have been paying attention, haven't you? Finally, I absolutely, thoroughly, completely love your plan. Don't know why I didn't think of it myself. We're going to have us a fine old time collecting all that stuff.

"Oh, and by the way, Olivia, in this neck of the woods, Appalachia is not pronounced 'Appa-*lay*-cha' as you just did. That's fingernails scrapping across a chalkboard to us. It is 'Appa-*lat*-cha' if you please."

"Got it, Forrest. 'Appa-lat-cha,' not 'Appa-lay-cha'; 'pop,' not 'soda'; and 'supper' is eaten at night and 'dinner' on Sunday afternoon. Am I making sufficient progress?"

"I reckon you're coming along."

Chapter Fourteen

Memories of Maggie Flood Forrest's Mind

Olivia's report from the investigators also has information about Maggie's daughter, Belinda, and it is so positive it practically glows. That good news, plus the unexpected information about her being a certified interior decorator two years out of college, prompts Forrest to have John Vermillion contact Belinda and set up a meeting with Bret to discuss the possibility of hiring her to be the on-site coordinator for the ritzy Chicago designers heading the project.

The idea of having Maggie's daughter helping with the renovation intrigues Forrest. He isn't certain about his motives though, so he ignores them.

What Forrest cannot ignore, no matter how hard he tries, are the memories of Maggie triggered by his imminent meeting with her daughter. He turns out the lights in his cabin, lets the darkness engulf him, and frees his mind to wander back to his first recollections of the girl he fell for with all his heart.

Forrest and Maggie first met in elementary school. But they paid little attention to each other because he and his friends thought that even though she was "kinda pretty," she was just a girl, and everybody knew girls weren't much fun to play with. Maggie and her friends had equal disdain for the boys at West Grade School because, after all, they were always "kinda dirty" and had no manners at all.

A big shock, however, was awaiting the guys when school resumed in the Fall between sixth and seventh grades. The first thing Forrest noticed when the graduates of West and other area elementary schools moved on to Asher Heights Junior High was the girls had undergone some sort of transformation that seemed to have passed the boys by.

Over the summer, Maggie, Caroline, and Misty and most of the others seem to have grown half a head taller than the boys, and their bodies were displaying some really fascinating stuff. The girls were developing into young women while Forrest and each of his baby-faced buddies were still straining mightily to force their bodies to squeeze out a couple of pubic hairs.

Mother Nature really is a bitch, they concluded. She has a Dirty Tricks Department and a wicked sense of humor.

Straining, however, was a word never applied to Maggie. By the time she was fourteen and in the ninth grade, she had the mature body of a grown woman. By anybody's reckoning she was stunning. And she damn well knew it and used it to her advantage at every opportunity.

Maggie had the flawlessly beautiful face and elegant movement of the dancer-actress Cyd Charisse and the body of a symmetrically slimmer Marilyn Monroe. She was five feet, five inches tall, weighed one hundred sixteen pounds, and her vital statistics were thirty-five, twenty-two, thirty-four.

Never one to miss a chance to put herself on display before helplessly libidinous adolescent males, Maggie yawned frequently, stretching her arms upward and back, a motion that thrust out her breasts to great advantage. Not to neglect her other favored features, she made exaggerated leans over tables to pick up a bottle of pop or to turn on a lamp, allowing her bottom to toot out like a freshly blooming morning glory.

She knew what she was doing. So did the boys. So did the teachers. But Maggie had thought through all the potential accusations. She was covered by *reasonable doubt*. After all, people yawn, people stretch, and people bend over. Lots of reasons for that.

After Mother Nature finally finished showering Maggie with generous attention, she managed to get around to Forrest in the ninth grade. He grew four inches in one year, stretching from five feet, four inches to five eight. He was shaving (a couple of times a week anyway), and his athletic body was muscular and fit. By his senior year in high school, he would become five more inches taller and weigh a hundred eighty-five pounds.

Forrest's dark brown hair and hazel eyes contrasted with Maggie's chestnut hair and lush eyebrows plucked to advantage to show off almond-shaped light green eyes beautifully displayed above an ideal straight-edged nose. Adorable dimples and full, passionate lips with a slight but permanent pucker showcased her sparkling white teeth and completed what was more of an artistic creation than a mere face.

Forrest was good-looking and had a chiseled body, but he was not Hollywood handsome. He had no trouble getting dates, but to his disappointment girls didn't swoon all over him. They were attracted to him, but they didn't melt in his presence.

However, considering Forrest as a whole, he had more appeal than the fairly generous looks he was born with. He was a top-notch student, fifth in his class of three hundred fourteen; he was a first-team letterman in football, baseball, and track; his fellow students elected him vice president of his senior class; he was chosen Most Likely to Succeed by the yearbook staff; and most fortunately where Maggie was concerned, he was a terrific dancer.

Like virtually all females in the history of humankind, Maggie loved dancing. The only thing she liked better was being beautiful and putting herself on public display. She liked Forrest all right, but he was not at the top of her must-date list. Fact was, none of Forrest's classmates could score big with Maggie because the older guys noticed her, too. And they had cars way before Forrest and his friends did. Besides, it was both flattering and exciting to be seen in the company of upperclassmen when she was a ninth and tenth grader, and college men when she was a high school senior.

Forrest had to content himself by creating a fantasy life with Maggie. He envisioned himself being greeted by her with open arms after scoring the winning touchdown in (why not? It was his fantasy) the state championship game. Or pairing with Maggie to win the jitterbug dance contest at the Senior Prom. Or driving around in his '57 Pontiac convertible (also a fantasy) on star-filled summer nights. And—dare he even dream it— making mad, passionate love in the back seat of his car with Maggie, safely hidden in the forests so easily accessible in New River County.

But that was fantasy; reality was something else. Forrest had persuaded Maggie to attend the Junior Prom with him, succeeding only because the older guys were banned by the strictly enforced non-student restriction, and she was not about to miss out on such an important event in her life. Besides, with Forrest she had the perfect partner for showing off her dancing skills. Maggie felt as if the world was hers to command. Or at least the male half of it.

Eventually, for reasons known only to herself, Maggie turned her attention fully on Forrest during their final semester of high school. In a miscalculation the perpetually scheming Maggie rarely made, she should have started one semester sooner. Had she done so, the senior boys would have dropped their resentment about her dating only college men and voted for her for Homecoming Queen or for the title of Miss Golden Eagle.

Maggie would have loved that, and it would have won her another prominent and permanent placement in the yearbook, a souvenir most of her classmates would keep for a lifetime. A missed opportunity. And Maggie rarely let those slip by.

Forrest's new class ring immediately moved from his finger to a gold chain around Maggie's neck, symbolizing two things: Maggie, with minimum effort, had pulled out of circulation one of the most popular boys in school, and Forrest had posted a clear sign that "his girl" was off limits.

Forrest had no pride where the alluring Maggie was concerned. He was as attentive and as faithful as a puppy and chauffeured her to and from anywhere her self-centered little heart desired to go. In return, Forrest was rewarded with superficial hugs and dry, lifeless kisses Maggie doled out in teasing trickles until she ever-so-slowly manipulated Forrest's passion to a fever pitch in time for the Senior Prom.

When that night arrived, Forrest, dressed uncomfortably in the first tuxedo he had ever worn, showed up promptly at six-thirty to present Maggie with an orchid corsage and escort her to the last big event before graduation. Predictably, Maggie was a knockout in an ice blue gown cut as low as the standards of the Board of Education would permit.

An afternoon at the beauty parlor having her hair fashioned in a classic updo style, and an hour in front of her bathroom mirror expertly applying makeup completed Maggie's meticulous preparations. The anticipated compliments started with her parents and would continue, Maggie was certain, throughout the evening. She was totally prepared to be viewed, wooed, and (although the entirely unsuspecting Forrest did not know it yet) made love to.

Unlike Forrest's friends and their dates, Maggie and Forrest skipped dinner. There was no way Maggie was going to chance spilling something on herself or disturbing her makeup. She also did not want to be seen by anyone until she made her grand entrance, predictably twenty minutes late to ensure she would have the full attention of classmates and teachers. Forrest felt uncomfortable in such a spotlight, but he was, after all, just a complementary prop for the triumphal appearance of the self-appointed Belle of the Ball.

With the energy of youth, Forrest and Maggie mixed, mingled, and danced nonstop, generously sharing themselves with other partners while the band played the musical hits of the day: "Wear My Ring Around Your Neck," by Elvis Presley; "Come Go With Me," by the Del-Vikings; Paul Anka's "You Are My Destiny"; "Sweet Little Sixteen," by Chuck Berry; Bobby Day's "Rock-in Robin"; "Hello, Young Lovers," by Johnny Mathis; "You Send Me," by Sam Cooke; Little Richard's "Lucille"; "Peggy Sue," by Buddy Holly; "All I have to Do Is Dream" by the Everly Brothers; Ray Charles's "What'd I Say"; and "Only You," by The Platters.

When the lights flickered at eleven p.m. to signal the close of the dance, the students, teachers, and chaperoning parents gathered in the middle of the school gym, joined hands to form a large unbroken circle and sang their alma mater, bringing a bitter-sweet end to the students' one-and-only Senior Prom, a singular moment whose memory, they would discover, increases in fondness with the passing of years.

But the closing of the prom did not necessarily signal the end of the evening. Many a young man was aware through locker-room lore that Senior Prom night provided the optimal opportunity for the shedding of one's virginity, males as well as females. Forrest was among the hopefuls.

To his surprise, Maggie gave him reason for the optimism that had prompted him for the first time since he was sixteen to replace the deteriorating pack of Trojans that had pressed a tell-tale circle into the leather wall of his wallet. She presented no resistance when he drove her to the secluded spot he had carefully staked out, just in case. He tuned the car radio to their favorite station, turned to Maggie and said, "We had a great time tonight, didn't we?"

"Oh, yes, Forrest," she replied, sliding to the middle of the front seat within his easy reach.

"You know you were the most beautiful girl there, Maggie. You also know how much I truly love you, don't you?'

"And I love you just as much, Forrest. But we've talked enough, don't you think? Why don't you show me how much you love me."

Forrest does not have to be invited twice. Even though he is scared to death his inexperience will make a fool of him, his passion overwhelms his anxiety. Nothing else in the world matters but Maggie and this moment. They kiss passionately, pressing tightly against each other.

Sensing Forrest's hesitation, Maggie make the first move for him, lifting his hand from her waist and sliding it breathtakingly slowly into place over her right breast while brushing her hand lightly back and forth over the upper inside of his left thigh, erasing all doubt that their moment has finally, after all of his previous unrewarded attempts, arrived.

It does not take long for Forrest to realize that although this is his first time, it isn't Maggie's. But at the moment that is of no importance to him. Nothing else is. He is about to have sex for the first time in his life with the girl literally of his dreams. Nothing can spoil that.

"Unzip me," she instructs with ragged breath, guiding Forrest to the next step and revealing perfectly shaped breasts much larger than he had imagined. Forrest moves his kisses from her lips and neck to enjoy what she has exposed.

"Meet me in the back seat?" Maggie whispers wetly into his ear. "And let's leave our clothes on the front seat. OK?"

"Oh, hell yes," Forrest gasps to himself, fumbling as fast as he can with buttons, belt, zipper, and shoestrings.

Maggie is already waiting, lying gloriously nude on the back seat, her irresistible, voluptuous body trembling with anticipation and clearly visible in the moonlight, arms stretched out invitingly. And although self-conscious to be so nakedly exposing his obvious state of excitement, Forrest positions his perfectly toned athletic body gently over hers, and in the next few rapturous moments, everything he had ever wished for with his breathtakingly seductive Maggie transforms from a fantasy into a memory of a lifetime.

Chapter Fifteen

Forrest Hires Maggie's Daughter

Although Forrest is eager and even a little nervous about meeting Maggie's daughter for the first time, he is genuinely innocent about how unprepared he is psychologically, emotionally, and in every other way for the impact she will have on him. The instant he sees Belinda, he feels as if Maggie herself is standing before him once again, but somehow contradictorily transformed.

He realizes how inadequate Olivia's description from the report is. It stressed that Belinda is nothing like her mother. The only thing they seem to have in common is their beauty. But even that is almost wholly different.

The young woman he is greeting is not stylish, as Maggie always was. Her hair is neatly brushed but not "fixed"; her skirt, blouse, and shoes look like a bank teller's uniform; she is wearing a faint amount of lipstick but no other makeup; her nails are neat and clean but clipped at the end of her fingers and unpolished; she wears no jewelry except for an inexpensive watch with large, easy-to-read numbers; and she walks in a manner that attracts no attention.

Maggie, on the other hand, always made a presentation of her appearance. Her hair looked as if she had just left a salon; her makeup was extensively but expertly applied; she wore jewelry, fashionable shoes, and the trendiest clothing; and her practiced walk was designed more to stimulate rubbernecked gawking than to get her from here to there. Altogether, the sight of her was intended to make other women, young and old, seethe with jealousy and to jump-start the erotic impulses of males of all ages.

Belinda also is two other things her mother was not at the age of twenty-three: deeply religious and a virgin. "Forrest, she is almost too good to be true," Olivia reported. "She doesn't smoke, drink, use drugs, or run around with the 'in crowd.' She teaches Sunday school to children and is the youngest member of the church council at First Baptist. She volunteers at the New River County Senior Citizens Center and is co-chair of the Asher Heights Times newspaper's annual Children's Christmas Toy Drive."

"Very impressive," Forrest told Olivia, thinking that surely Belinda must do something for fun, and inquired about her personal life?"

"She dates occasionally with nice young men," the report indicated, but no serious relationship so far. "She is a huge fan of old black-and-white movies from the thirties and forties. Loves Bette Davis films, and adores musicals with Fred Astaire, Ginger Rogers, Rita Hayworth, Donald O'Connor, Gene Kelly, Ann Miller, and the Nicholas Brothers. And, like her mother, she is a skillful dancer.

"And she devours comic books about superheroes like Superman, Batman, Wonder Woman, and Captain Marvel, probably because they fight for good against evil."

Olivia put off talking about Belinda's being a decorator. Knowing Forrest as well as she does, Olivia has a dreadful feeling he might want to work with her, but she is worried about why. Would it be to help set Maggie up for the crushing news of Forrest's great success and his moving back to town to overwhelm her and everyone else with his tremendous wealth? Or is it because of the reaction she saw on Forrest's face when she showed him the picture the investigators provided? Would working with Belinda somehow make her a substitute for her mother, who was about Belinda's age when she called off the wedding?

Whatever the reason, it nags at Olivia, but she knows there is nothing she can do about it. Forrest had convinced himself even before the meeting that Belinda will do an inspired job of carrying out his plans for the meditation room/chapel.

Forrest puts the report out of his mind and takes a close look at the young woman as Belinda approaches him with her hand extended.

He sees Belinda's obvious efforts to hide her beauty fail her. "God, you are beautiful," Forrest, still presenting himself as Bret Doyle, blurts out, embarrassing both himself and Belinda.

"Sorry, Ms. Bottoms. I did not intend to be rude; that remark just slipped out unintentionally. Please accept it as a compliment, along with my apologies."

"Certainly, sir," a blushing Belinda responds in a friendly tone. "And, please, call me Belinda."

"I will if you will call me Bret. After all, we will be working closely together until this project of ours is finished quite some time from now."

As they go over the preliminary details involving her credentials, her areas of expertise, and her availability, Forrest has trouble concentrating. Despite his efforts to the contrary, his mind is racing with ideas—not all of them to his liking.

He didn't intend to have such a strong attraction to Belinda. She is so very different from her mother; yet, God evidently used the same mold when he formed her. Against his will, he senses the feelings he had for Maggie transferring to Belinda, who is almost as young as Maggie was when she left him.

Parts of Forrest he thought had died years ago are springing to life as Belinda unwittingly reignites the embers of romantic passion Maggie doused so long ago. Irrational possibilities form in his mind. Could he love this young woman? Could he cause her to love him? Could the marriage and children Maggie cheated him out of when she broke his heart be made right by Belinda?

Forrest feels like a cartoon character he remembers seeing with a tiny angel perched on one shoulder whispering righteous instructions into his right ear while a miniature devil stands on his left shoulder and temps his dark side, saying: "Marrying Belinda would be the ultimate revenge against Maggie. It's perfect, Forrest. You get a beautiful young woman you have the money to treat like a princess while her mother is locked in an unhappy union with a man she does not even like, much less love.

"Maggie has money, and the things money can buy, but she is not happy, has no romance or passion in her life—all of which she could have had with you if she had not chosen 'Mr. Loser' over you. And, best of all by far, Forrest, your children will be her *grandchildren!*

"It's taken you more than two decades, Forrest, but the time and the opportunity and the circumstances are perfect. Make Maggie pay for all the suffering she has put you through. You'll never get a better chance."

Forrest feels like clapping his hands over his ears and shouting out the voices, good and bad. But with a mighty effort, he calms himself and hurriedly explains to Belinda he has a conference call he must attend to. They agree to meet again the next day.

Chapter Sixteen

A Guilty Conscience

Over the next several months, as Forrest works with Belinda, he becomes convinced she is a genuinely good young woman. From the permanent harm done him by Maggie to his many business experiences with people who seem to be one thing and turn out to be quite another, Forrest has learned to protect himself and his judgment with a healthy dose of skepticism. He wanted Belinda to be as good as the investigators' reports indicated, but he had to see it for himself. And now that he has, he is a believer.

"Belinda, the man we are doing all this work for wants to give you some more responsibility if you are willing. Some of it is directly related to the design and decorating we hired you for, specifically coming up with a priority list to complete the subjects for the stained-glass panels in the chapel. He's giving you an open budget to contact, talk with, travel if necessary, whatever. He wants at least one panel with children and the others to incorporate all races of religious people from around the world.

"The new duties would be more in the area of public relations. He wants to help the community accomplish some things that finances may be keeping the good people here from doing."

"Like what, Bret? I mean, it sounds wonderful, but did he mention any specifics?"

"Only generally, Belinda. Because you are a lifelong resident of Asher Heights and New River County, he figures you are sufficiently connected to talk with the appropriate people and come up with a 'wish list.' Some things like, but not limited to, school needs such as buses, band uniforms, scholarships, and community essentials like police cars, ambulances, fire trucks, anything that can be done for senior citizens, a food bank, and so forth. Will that help you get started, presuming you are willing to take on this project?"

"Bret, I've prayed all my life that God would give me meaningful work to do for His people. This won't be just a job for me; it will be a calling. I am so grateful, I can't wait to get started. Is there a timetable?"

"No, not really. But I am aware that our employer is impatient once he gets a notion to do something. To help you get started, I can tell you he wants to establish five college scholarships for Asher Heights seniors, and when the time is right, he will make known the names of the people he wants the scholarships to honor."

"I'm on it, Bret. Tell him thank you for me, and assure him I will not let him down."

***

Forrest's motives are not altogether altruistic. He's suffering from a sizable case of a guilty conscience. He is plagued by Olivia's warning that his reasons for spending millions of dollars on that old mansion and moving back to Asher Heights may just be an excuse for revenge. That, plus being subjected every day to Belinda's continual references to religion, makes him feel God is watching him spend a fortune selfishly on himself instead of how The Almighty would have him devote his money where it would do more good.

So, Forrest determines also to spend additional millions benefiting mankind, hoping that will balance out his other plans, which he is not about to abandon, but now hopes he can continue to pursue minus the guilt. Forrest's belief in God and in Heaven, as sincere as it is, has always come, for some reason he has never understood, anchored to a ball-and-chain of nagging guilt further weighted down by a mix of superstition. He continually questions whether his numerous acts of generosity are in answer to God's call or are in response to his fear of retribution against either him or someone dear to him if he ignores the needs of his fellow man. Makes him wish he had never read about the wrath of God in the Old Testament.

Anyway, Forrest avoids the risk. He gives generously. Maybe the evangelist Billy Graham knew the answers to such dilemmas, Forrest reasons, but he himself has long accepted that he does not and never will.

Chapter Seventeen

Belinda Tells Maggie about Her Mansion Job

One of Belinda's rare failings is always expecting the best of other people. It is a commendable fault—if such a contradictory quality is possible—that unfairly blindsides those who are thoroughly good and sincerely religious. It causes Belinda to err when she tells her mother about being hired as a decorator for Old Mrs. Kimble's mansion.

Instead of the congratulations Belinda innocently expects, Maggie jumps all over the opportunity to further her personal interests in prying into the identity of the mansion's new owner. Belinda realizes too late she has made a mistake, one that could cost her the new job if Maggie interferes to the point that Bret Doyle fires her. He warned her in the clearest of English how absolute the requirement of secrecy must be.

"Who is the new owner, Belinda?" Maggie demands, not asks.

"I do not know, Mother, and there is no chance I am going to be told voluntarily. And why is that so important to you? I only told you about the job because I thought you would be happy for me, getting such a big opportunity in only my second year in the business."

"Oh, I am proud of you, my love," Maggie hastily adds while giving Belinda a superficial hug, recognizing that if she is to get any information out of her daughter, she will have to be more discreet and tactful.

"Tell me, dear, who is it that hired you?"

"His name is Bret Doyle, and he is the new owner's on-site representative."

"And what is it, specifically, he asked you to do. Belinda?"

"I can't go into details about that, Mother. But my role is significant, and maybe after the owner eventually makes his identity known, I can show you the results of what I have done."

"I would like that very much," Maggie responds, her perpetually scheming mind plotting ways she can find out much more before the owner is ready to reveal himself. "Mr. Doyle must be a little lonely, honey, being a stranger and all. Nat and I would be glad to have him over for dinner."

Belinda isn't that naïve. She made certain her mother knew that was not going to happen. Bret had warned Belinda and everyone else he dealt with, he wanted no one trying to use him to unveil the identity of the owner. It would be a firing offense, he emphasized.

With the failure of that tactic, Maggie backs off, says an abrupt good-bye by placing a quick kiss on Belinda's cheek and rushes her daughter out the door. Maggie has other plans to get the information she craves, including how to make an I-just-happened-to-be-in-the-neighborhood drop-in at the mansion.

Chapter Eighteen

LeRoy Reaches Out to Belinda

Belinda's relationship with her mother is far less than ideal, and her contact with her father is rare. He never writes or remembers a birthday or any other significant occasion. So, she is taken aback when she gets his telephone call.

"Hi, Dad. What a surprise to get a ring from you after being out of touch for—how long has it been this time? More than a year?"

"Belinda, I'm sorry I changed telephone numbers without tellin' yuh, as well as not contactin' yuh fer so long. I won't give yuh no excuses. I'm sure yuh've memorized all my usual ones. Anyhow, I got somethin' I want tuh tell yuh, but only in person. Can we meet fer a meal or a long walk somewhur?"

"Sounds mysterious, Dad, and I'm curious. How about breakfast at seven thirty tomorrow at the Wishbone Café?"

"Ok. See yuh thur."

Belinda hangs up with some anxiety. Contact between her and her father is infrequent, to put it kindly, and she is always the initiator. That has her worried because he never has positive news beyond his next strike-it-rich pipe dream that never advances beyond the blather stage.

"Something very different is up, I think. I pray it is not as bad as I fear."

***

After their usual awkward greeting and they have placed their orders,

LeRoy comes right out with it. No build up. No preparation. No attempt to soften the message.

"Belinda, I'm dyin' from lung cancer. The doctors gimme a year or two at most. And, yeah, I have had a second opinion. And a third and a fourth. Thur's no question 'bout how bad it is."

Belinda stares numbly at her father, giving herself time to allow her rationality to overcome her understandably emotional reaction to such stunningly dreadful news. "I'm so sorry, Dad. You're only forty-seven years old. I wasn't prepared to hear this."

"Well, after I had time tuh get used tuh the outlook, I really wasn't so surprised. I never took good care of myself. Smoked like a chimney since I was fourteen; drank at least a pint of whiskey a day; sniffed up my nose everthang I could get my hands on . . . It's a wonder I've lasted this long, yuh know?"

Belinda does know. He is undoubtedly the most reckless, irresponsible, undependable person she had ever known. But in spite of it all, she somehow manages to love him. "Honor they father," she has reminded herself countless times in her prayers.

"What are you going to do, Dad? Where are you living? Do you have any income? Do—"

"Whoa thur, little missy. I'm all right. I moved back tuh Asher Heights three months ago. Didn't want tuh see yuh or talk tuh yuh 'til I knowed fer certain about my condition. I'm livin' with Aunt Willa. Yuh know, Willa Dunkle, my late mother's sister. She always had a soft spot fer me, even after your grandmother finally kicked me outta the house. Willa has a decent income and I'm on disability, so we have enough.

"Hope me and you can use somma thuh time tuh finally git tuh know each other better, Belinda. It's all my fault we don't, but I'd like tuh do what I can with the time I have left if yer willin'."

"Of course, I'm willing, Dad. But I must warn you, I live my life for Christ, so I'll be doing everything I can to help you save your soul. I must. The Lord would not guide me any other way."

"I don't know how much yuh can do in so short a time 'cause I have an awful lot tuh answer fer. And most of it, I'd just as soon yuh not know 'bout me. But I'll do anythang to spend time with yuh durin' this last period of my life."

"I'm just an instrument of the Lord's, Dad. And it takes only a moment of genuine sincerity and acceptance for Him to save you. The Bible is full of His miracles, you know."

"Well, it's gonna take a doozy to forgive all I done. But I'll sincerely try. I promise yuh that."

For the first time in her life, Belinda believes her father intends to keep his word.

Chapter Nineteen

Forrest Tells Belinda His True Identity

As the massive reconstruction project draws to a close and with the decorating almost complete, Forrest cannot put off much longer revealing to Belinda the identity of the owner. She would never understand why her mother could not finally "drop in" and check out the place to her heart's content. Much more importantly, Forrest could not subject Belinda to the inestimable harm that surely would occur if she found out any other way the owner's identity and especially what her mother had done to him.

"Belinda," Forrest begins as he closes the library door behind her, "I am going to reveal to you the identity of the owner. I promised you I would just before he was going to make it known publicly himself. But you do understand, of course, you are to tell no one until after he does."

"Of course, Bret. That's perfectly understandable, and I think you know you can count on my discretion."

"I do, Belinda. I want you to know that during all these months we've worked closely together, I've come to trust you more than I have trusted anyone else since I've been an adult. But you are going to have to trust me even more than you have during our working relationship. I'm very worried that you will have ill feelings toward me and—"

"Oh, no, Bret," Belinda interrupts. "You've been so easy to work with, and I could never repay you enough for your patience and guidance. I can't imagine what you're concerned about."

"Well, you're about to find out, my precious friend. Please, promise me you won't bolt out of the room. You must allow me to explain in detail. I could not live with myself if you do not fully hear me out."

"Are you telling me I should be frightened, Bret?'

"No, not at all, Belinda. It's a matter of trust, not fear.

"Belinda, my name is not Bret Doyle, and I am not the owner's representative. *I am the owner.*"

Belinda is speechless. She looks faint. Her eyes are as wide open as her mouth, but her mind will not allow her tongue to give voice to the logjam of words trying to burst out. All she can manage to utter is "Why?!"

"Why, Belinda? Because I wanted to be on site while everything was being done. I've waited almost a quarter of a century to purchase the mansion, and I just could not stand not being here to oversee the work."

"But why was it so important not to reveal your name, whatever it is? What harm would that have done?"

"I'm getting to that, Belinda. It's a long, involved story, and it affects you very personally. That's the main reason I hired you to work with me even though you had little experience. And, by the way, you've done a terrific job. I could not be more pleased.

"Here is the big shock. I hope you can assimilate all of it and find it in your heart to forgive me if you feel I have wronged you. My name is Forrest Alderson, and I was born and grew up right here in Asher Heights. I've loved this old mansion since I was a boy and always dreamed of one day owning it, ever since I was a kid from a family that had very little money, and I had no realistic prospects of ever buying this place.

"You've never seen me in Asher Heights before because I left when I was twenty-one, months before you were born, and I never returned until I was ready to buy the mansion. And before you ask, let me tell you why. Belinda, this is the personal part, so please try to understand.

"Your mother, Maggie McDaniel Mullens, and I went together in high school and throughout college and were to be married. She broke off our engagement one week before the wedding, and I couldn't handle it.

It's more complicated than I care to tell you, but I cut my ties with Asher Heights and everyone in it, including my best friends.

"I took off to Chicago and vowed to do nothing but make enough money to one day return home and buy this mansion. I made a great deal of money, Belinda. I do not expect you to understand because I do not fully understand precisely why myself. My attorney and friend, Olivia Fillmore, fears I may be doing this to show Maggie what a gigantic mistake she made by not marrying me. That may be true. The truth is I do not know.

"Nevertheless, here I am today. I'm enormously wealthy; I own my dream mansion and it's everything I wanted it to be. But what my next step is, I have no clue.

"That's pretty much it, Belinda, so please say something. I won't have any peace of mind until you do. Either we'll carry on as friends, or you may shun me forever. Either way, I've got to know."

"Oh, Forrest, I don't know quite what to say except I assure you I am neither angry nor feel misused. What I do feel is great confusion. I need to do a lot of thinking, and I'm sure I'll want to know as many details about your relationship with my mother as you are willing to tell me. But that can come later. For right now, I have a few questions I'd like answers to, if it's OK with you."

"Anything, Belinda. Ask anything."

"You really, truly loved my mother? And if she also loved you as you said, why did she break things off right before the wedding?"

"I loved your mother with every fiber of my being. So much so, I've not only never married anyone else, I've never even had a serious relationship since Maggie left me. As to why, I think you should hear that from her, if she is willing to tell you. All I will say is it involved your father."

"My last question for now, Forrest, is when can I tell mother who you are and ask her about the circumstances of the breakup? And I hope you realize she probably will give me a one-sided picture, so I'll have to come back to you to get your point of view. Is that OK?"

"Perfectly. I'll let you know when. And it will be soon."

"Still friends?" Forrest earnestly asks, his eyes all but begging for Belinda's blessing.

"Yes, Forrest. Do not let your mind be troubled. Let's just put all of this in God's hands. He fully understands, even when we don't. Let's pray He will guide us. He never fails us if we just take a moment to ask.

"Thank you for confiding in me, Forrest. I'm going to be a little muddle-minded for a while," she smiles. "But so will you, I suspect. And God only knows how mother will react."

Chapter Twenty

Belinda Shocks Her Mother

Unlike many other believers, Belinda has no set time for prayer. Not every morning or just before bedtime or once a week in church. As long as she can remember, she has carried on a continual conversation with God. Sometimes it is just a sentence such as "Give me strength," or "Give me guidance," or "Help me to understand," or "Show me what I must do." Sometimes, it's just a few words of gratitude such as "Thank you, Lord," or "You're so good to us, Father," or "Thank you for keeping us safe." Belinda shares with God whatever she is feeling or thinking at the moment.

But this day is different. This time Belinda asks for forgiveness in advance, for this is the day she is going to tell her mother not only what Maggie has wanted to know for months but also stunning details Maggie is totally unprepared to hear. Belinda asks for forgiveness because she is ashamed to be human enough to be eager to see how her mother reacts in one of those extremely rare instances in which Maggie herself is not in command.

* * *

"The new owner is who?!!!" Maggie shrieks.

"You heard right, Mother. It's Forrest Alderson. The man you were supposed to marry."

"And you knew all along and have been keeping this from me for more than a year!"

"No, mother, the man I knew as Bret Doyle waited until the mansion was finished before telling me, and I came over here as soon as he told me I was free to tell you.

"Time for a rare mother-daughter talk, wouldn't you agree?"

"I guess so, Belinda. But only if you will tell me every detail. And don't you dare leave out a single syllable. Oh, and when do I get to see the house?"

Belinda can't suppress a laugh, the question is so typical of her self-centered mother. "Believe it or not, Forrest has given me permission to take you on a tour. But you're getting a little ahead of yourself, don't you think."

"Don't move an inch from that chair, Belinda. Not until you've answered every question. Start with what Forrest looks like. No, scratch that. Start with where he got all his money. The last time I saw him, he had just graduated from college and hardly had two nickels to rub together."

"Well, try to calm your avaricious little heart, mother. You might need a valium pill after you hear this. Forrest may have been broke the last time you saw him, but I've heard he's now worth somewhere between one hundred million and two hundred million dollars!"

Maggie is stunned. Dumbstruck.

"You heard right, Mother. I'm not kidding."

"Where in the world did he get so much money? He's not one of those notorious Chicago gangsters, is he?"

"No," Belinda giggles. "Big-time Chicago real estate, mother. He owned his own company, one of the biggest in the city."

"Whew!" Maggie exhales. "I think I've recovered enough to ask what he is doing back here in little Asher Heights? Why did he buy that old mansion? What's he up to?"

"We may find out; we may not. He's very private."

"OK, now tell me what he looks like. Please say time has been terrible to him. That he looks sixty, is losing his hair, and has a big pot belly."

Belinda's spontaneous laugh answers her mother's questions. "He's trim, fit, appears to have all of his own teeth, has a full head of hair, beautiful eyes, and a great tan. And he's really nice on top of all that. I find him quite attractive."

Maggie detects a sparkle in her daughter's eyes that she does not like.

"Not too attractive I hope, Belinda. You don't have a thing for him, do you?"

"I could, mother. He has taken me to lunch and dinner a number of times. I know he likes me. And I think he understands me because he sometimes looks at me as if he has known me forever."

Alarm bells go off loudly and clearly in Maggie's head, ringing a warning that only a person who has led a life of cunning and deceit is wired to recognize.

"Belinda, you cannot get romantically involved with Forrest," she pleads.

"And why not, mother? Are you referring to the age difference? My lack of experience with men? Perhaps an interest you still have in him?"

"Listen to me carefully, my daughter. I'm going to have the most honest talk with you we've ever had. Our only real one we've had woman-to-woman. I don't think jealousy has any part in this, although I will admit I was deeply in love with Forrest way back when.

"Your inexperience is part of it. His age is part of it. But what I fear most is he may be after you to get back at me for the great hurt I did to him and for which I'm all but certain he's never gotten over. Think about this: You said he's never gotten married. He's moved back to a town he has intentionally avoided since our breakup. He has maintained no relationships here with anybody. And for reasons I can't even imagine, he has bought an old mansion and is spending millions to restore it.

"If he's sending me a message that I screwed up royally by not marrying him, I get it loudly and clearly. I admit it. I chose a clunker over a Rolls-Royce. Forrest may not want to concede this to me, but I've also suffered dearly for that colossal mistake and so have you, Belinda."

"But isn't it possible, Mother, that Forrest likes me for just being me and that it has nothing to do with you?"

"Possible but very improbable, my darling. Please understand that I love and admire the fact that you are such an honest, religious, thoroughly good person. You are not like your father and me. I have no idea where you got those qualities unless it was from my mother, who is much like you in so many ways.

"But your goodness comes with a major flaw. Your very trust and belief in the fundamental goodness of the human race makes you vulnerable. I'll just say it, Belinda: You are naive. Other girls your age, girls who've had romantic, sexual relationships with several men, would be very much on guard in your situation."

"I still think I may be right, Mother. Shouldn't I at least give myself a chance to see where this relationship leads? That is if I have that kind of relationship at all. I could be reading too much into this, you know."

Sensing she is losing her attempt to save her daughter from a mistake that could have a lifetime of heartbreaking consequences, Maggie takes a deep breath, says a rare prayer, and plays her hole card.

"Sweetheart, I am going to tell you something you should have figured out on your own, but because of your innocence, I'm afraid you have not. But it's something you must factor into your considerations."

Belinda can read the trepidation on her mother's face. It's something she has never before witnessed. "Mother, I'm not sure I want to hear this, but I suppose I must."

"Then, prepare yourself, Belinda. It's not something I would ever have brought up if Forrest had not moved back here and shown an interest in you. I think the one thing that makes it impossible for a moral young woman like you to marry Forrest is this: *"Could you ever in good conscience sleep with a husband who has had sex many times with your own mother?!"*

* * *

Maggie leaves her meeting with Belinda literally nauseated, her self-esteem suffering from the realization that her relationship with Belinda is upside down. Instead of her being a role model for her daughter, as all good mothers are, it's Belinda who sets the example for her!

And Maggie has just admitted to her virtuous daughter how unvirtuous she herself was at a much younger age than Belinda is now. Only one other time in her life has Maggie forced herself to face the unvarnished reality about her character and the choices she had made, and that was when she finally realized the truth about LeRoy Bottoms.

"I can't dwell on this now," Maggie chastises herself. "I must find out what Forrest is up to. What his real designs are, if any, on Belinda? Did I shock her enough with my confession to put an end to any possibility of a serious relationship between them? Should I confront Forrest?"

For one of the few times in her life, Maggie's confidence fails her. She is—at least temporarily—stumped.

Chapter Twenty-One

Olivia Gives Forrest an Ultimatum

In the year and a half it has taken to complete work on the mansion, Olivia and Forrest have communicated almost daily and gotten together regularly, usually in Asher Heights but also half a dozen times or so for weekend vacations to wherever they take a notion to go. With Forrest's kind of money, no accommodations are impossible, even last-minute ones.

Olivia has long been convinced Forrest is the man she could be happy with for a lifetime, and it's obvious to her he not only enjoys but loves being with her. No man has ever treated her with more kindness, attentiveness, and generosity. From the moment she first met him, she has considered him worth the investment of her love.

She thinks, but is frustratingly uncertain, he looks upon her the same way. He continually compliments her on her judgment, her insightfulness, her intelligence, and her sense of humor. And she has noticed— because she has taken pains to do so—the longing in his eyes when he has seen her beautifully shaped body exposed at the beach. She has felt the beating of his heart and his pronounced breathing when they embrace. But he has yet to make love to her, and she has presented him with many opportunities.

However, as much as she cares for him, her patience is nearing an end. She is forty-two years old and has no desire to live the remainder of her life alone. She has continued to date, and Forrest knows it. Furthermore, she believes he must know she is still occasionally sexually active —just as he undoubtedly is with those courtesans he has substituted for a real love life.

She has reached the edge for two reasons. For one, her work on the mansion, a true labor of love, has neared its end. All that is left is assisting Forrest in planning a couple of parties to celebrate. The second is what happened when they last vacationed together.

Since the time he confessed his fears to her about entering a romantic relationship, she has been extremely careful in how fast and how far she pushed him. But after months passed without any advancement in that part of their relationship, she figured it was time to abandon that strategy.

They kissed regularly, walked hand in hand and arm in arm everywhere they went, and shared other moments of affection. But that's as far as things progressed. They even shared the same bed a couple of times when they made plans so late only a single-bed accommodation was available.

That was the case at their last meeting when she made her move— one designed to lift their relationship to the level it should have reached long ago, or possibly to end it altogether.

Forrest already was in bed, wearing pajamas and lying as far to the edge of the mattress as he could get. She joined him a few minutes later, minus any clothing at all. The lights were off, and Forrest had his eyes closed, not noticing her nudity until he leaned over to kiss her good night.

"It's time, Forrest" she said invitingly but firmly.

"You're right, Olivia," he said, just as firmly, wrapping her in his arms and kissing her, gently at first but increasingly passionately as their hands roamed the other's body, touching intimately as they never had before. "There's nothing wrong with his lovemaking skills," she quickly concludes. But as her hand touches him most intimately, she realizes with depressing disappointment he is not.

He backed away, lay on his back, hands folded behind his head, and said nothing. He wanted to become invisible and disappear. Here he was, in bed with the most wonderful woman he had ever known. Beautiful.

Desirable. Extraordinarily kind and understanding. And he couldn't manage to be man enough to fully express his love for her.

"Saying I'm sorry is so inadequate, Olivia. I wish I could simply vanish I am so embarrassed and humiliated. Please, please know, it's not because I do not want you. I'm crazy with desire for you."

Mincing no words, Olivia did not ask but ordered: "Let's get past all of that, Forrest. I believe you, but we can't just let it go at that or we will inevitably go our separate ways. I think I know what you must do if you want to advance our relationship.

"I've thought about this for a long time. I'm no psychologist or psychiatrist, but I don't have to be either to know you will never be able to be intimate with any woman other than prostitutes if you do not confront Maggie in person and have it out with her once and for all. That's the only way you stand a chance at overcoming what she did to you all those years ago.

"The question is, will you do that? Are you capable of doing that? And immediately. As soon as you get back home."

"I can and I will, Olivia. You have my word. Tonight has pushed me beyond my limits. I won't live like this any longer. I can't tolerate living like this. We both deserve to know, finally and for good, if I can break loose or if I'm doomed."

***

Reality is indeed such a personal concept, Olivia reasons. She and Forrest (and undoubtedly Maggie) have such vastly different conceptions of what the ramifications are or should be of the broken engagement more than twenty years later. Everyone lives in his or her own reality, she concludes. And reality exists between each person's ears.

Chapter Twenty-Two

The Reunion of Forrest and Maggie

Forrest keeps his word. Even though he has misgivings—and to his considerable annoyance, a large dose of anxiety—he enlists Belinda's cooperation in drawing Maggie to the mansion for a tour she presumes will take place in Forrest's absence. Belinda initially declines Forrest's request because she considers deception to be morally wrong. But he convinces her that her mother is more likely to be honest if she is caught off guard.

Belinda complies, and as she ushers Maggie into the mansion, she gives no indication her mother is there for anything other than a tour.

"Mother, I've saved Forrest's library for last because it's his most private room, and he doesn't let anyone in without his permission, which he has given me. Go ahead and look around while I go to the bathroom."

Belinda has trouble telling even little white lies, so she goes to the bathroom as she said she would. She knows Forrest has allowed the tour so he can see and talk with Maggie for the first time since the night she broke his heart. Belinda did not lie; she simply let her mother presume Forrest was not at home.

As she enters the room, Maggie again is overwhelmed, just as she has been with the magnificent restoration and decoration of the rest of the mansion she already has toured. Except for the extraordinary stained-glass windows, almost everything else in the library is made of wood. Everything from the floor of American chestnut from trees that later became extinct to the maple walls and bookshelves. The glossy rosewood desk is such a contrast, it attracts Maggie's eye almost immediately.

It holds her attention for only an instant, however, because seated in the chair behind it is the man she has not seen since that fateful night so long ago. It takes all her strength not to collapse as the blood drains from her face and her heart threatens to quit pumping life through her veins.

Forrest forbade Belinda from telling her mother he would be in the library. He wanted an honest reaction from Maggie, and he knew darned good and well that's not what he would have gotten if she had been forewarned and had had time to put together an advantageous scheme.

"Maggie Mullens," Forrest barely whispers.

"Forrest Alderson," Maggie gasps!

When she is able to speak, Maggie says, "You have the advantage of me, Forrest. If I had known you were home, I doubt I would have had the courage to come, as curious as I've been to see you since Belinda told me you are the mystery man who bought the mansion."

Forrest says nothing, letting silence fill the space between them. All he has done is stand, as any gentleman would.

"For God's sake, Forrest, say something. I don't know whether you want to talk to me or kill me. I can't stop you from doing either one, so I'll have a seat before my legs give out from under me. Anyway, the next move is yours."

Forrest's voice may not have been active, but his mind is racing to assimilate all the information his eyes and ears are sending him. Maggie, without a doubt, is still beautiful. As always, her hair, makeup, clothing, and jewelry are impeccable. Yet, something is fundamentally different, and trying to figure out what it is has kept him from speaking.

Maggie looks older, of course. So does he. She has taken on a few more pounds. So has he. Her hair is a little darker, probably from having it colored. His is about half gray. Maybe the fundamental difference he detected is not physical. If not that, then what? Perhaps, he will figure out the answer as they talk.

"You don't need to fear me, Maggie. For a time after you left me, I considered doing away with both of us. But that was many years ago. I've had a long time to sort things out, but I must admit, I still haven't been able to do that completely.

"I suppose my most nagging question all these years is *why?* I loved you. I was faithful to you. I was dedicated to marrying you and spending the rest of my life with you. Please tell me why. Did I do something wrong? Did I fail to do something I should have done? You have no conception of how those questions have haunted me, Maggie."

Maggie answers truthfully with no attempt at deception. "You did nothing wrong, Forrest. And there was nothing you failed to do. I am solely at fault. I can blame no one else except perhaps poetic justice, payback for all the hearts I broke from the time I was fourteen years old.

"I, too, have done a great, great deal of thinking and soul searching since I last saw you. And I have reached some conclusions without knowing for sure whether they are right or wrong. So, without regard to modesty or immodesty, let me put it this way.

"My beauty has been both a gift and a curse. From the age of fourteen, I've been aware of the power I've held over boys at first and then men. I saw the looks I got, the direct ones and the hidden ones, and I used them to my advantage. It did not take me long to learn that it wasn't just guys my age who wanted me, but males of all ages—even the very good ones like uncles and cousins and people who saw me only in church. They would never have acted on it, but they desired me all the same.

"From the time I first had a mature body until I messed up my life with LeRoy Bottoms, I knew I could have any guy I wanted. Including you, Forrest. I know how arrogant and conceited that sounds, but I am telling the truth. I had the control, and like everyone else inexperienced and young, I couldn't see any end to it. I thought what I had would last forever.

"Then along came seductively handsome LeRoy Bottoms, and he was very, very different from any guy of my experience. He read me like a book that he knew oh so well from all the other silly, gullible girls he'd taken advantage of before. He almost immediately reversed my 'advantage.' Even though I was much more intelligent than he was, he had 'street smarts,' something that in my sheltered life I knew nothing about.

"He was crude, vulgar, and unprincipled. And he purposely played me by acting as if I were as plain as a piece of white bread. I took up the challenge, certain he couldn't resist me, but I was in over my head almost immediately. That started the retribution I so richly deserved for not caring about the feelings of countless guys whose emotions I toyed with liked a cat with a mouse. It never occurred to me to consider the hurt I was causing.

"I had to have LeRoy, but as he counted on, the only way I could do that was with sex. I gave in, and I was hooked. I was so overwhelmed I abandoned you, my family and friends, my teaching career. Everything. I knew I was doing something totally destructive, but I was so in love — and so in lust I'll admit while I'm being truthful—I literally did not give a damn at that moment about anyone or anything else. By the time reality came crashing down on me, it was too late. I was divorced. I had a child. And I was disgraced.

"Not marrying you, Forrest, was the biggest mistake in my life. And it is still having its consequences on both of us. Now, it's your turn to talk while I listen. Why did you come back after all these years? What does this mansion mean to you? What do you want?"

"Maggie, I'm not precisely sure why I came back and bought and restored this place. I went to Chicago to get away from you and everybody and everything that reminded me of you. I also went there to do the only thing I could think of that gave me the will to go on living. And that was making all the money I could as fast as I could and buying this mansion.

And that's what I did. What I was going to do after that, I never thought about; I just did it."

"Apparently, you more than succeeded, Forrest. Belinda told me you are worth as much as two hundred million dollars."

"Much more, Maggie. And because what you did to me put me on that path, I'll tell you something no one else other than my tax attorney knows. It's closer to a billion dollars.

"A good friend of mine thinks I did all of this to come back to Asher Heights and rub my wealth and my success in your face, Maggie. Maybe it's my way of getting even with you, although if it is, it doesn't come near to making up for the suffering your leaving caused me."

"Forrest, if it makes any difference, I'll tell you I, too, have suffered because of what I did, and so unfortunately has my daughter. I haven't been truly happy since I faced the fact that I threw my life away over a man who doesn't have a single one of your good qualities.

"After LeRoy, I deceived into marrying me a rich man I never loved, and now we're both miserable. I console myself by spending his money and taking vacations to get away from him, and he works all the time to avoid having to deal with me. The only good that's come of our marriage is our son, and the fact Nat loves Belinda as much as if she were his biological daughter. He's essentially a very good human being, Forrest, but I cannot tolerate intimacy with him."

"Tell me, Maggie. In all of that mess, how did Belinda turn out to be the extraordinarily good young woman she is?"

"God's grace is all I can figure, Forrest. That and perhaps the influence of my mother, who has spent as much time raising Belinda as I have. I know you probably thought my mother was just a silly woman, but she is as genuinely good as Belinda. And she is very religious; that's where Belinda gets her devotion to the Lord. Wish more of it would rub off on me.

"One last thing, Forrest. I'm afraid Belinda may be infatuated with 'Bret' and now you. You have every right to hurt me back for what I did to you to keep you from trusting another woman enough to get married and have children and a normal life, but please don't pursue Belinda and ruin her life to punish me. Surely, you haven't changed so much from the decent man I knew that you'd use her against me."

"To be honest, I thought about it, Maggie. I know there's nothing else I could do to hurt you more. Perhaps if she had turned out to be more like you, I could have done it. But not after getting to know her. Everything she does appeals to the best instincts of others, including me. She needs to marry someone who values a religious life as much as she does.

"Put your mind at ease about Belinda. I swear I will never harm her in any way. Fact is, she is well on her way to improving me."

"So where does that leave us, Forrest? If we both stay in this town, we can't totally avoid running into each other."

"How about settling for just being civil, Maggie?"

"That I can do."

* * *

At some point during their talk, Forrest found the answer for the fundamental difference he detected when he first looked at Maggie. It is the total loss of her youthful innocence. After her experiences of the past twenty-some years, she has no purity left. She is still beautiful, but she has visibly "hardened."

The adorable pout of her teenage lips has been replaced by a clinched mouth that rarely forms a smile. The hopeful sparkle Forrest had loved in her eyes has been dulled by the somberness of reality. There is no spontaneity, no gaiety, no lightheartedness. Maggie has flamed out far too quickly. All of her softness and tenderness has burned away.

She spent the first two decades of her life flouting every rule and every convention that didn't suit her purpose and the next two decades paying dearly for it.

Forrest has no need to inflict his revenge upon Maggie. The hell she has already brought upon herself surpasses any suffering he had wished upon her.

* * *

If any chance remains that Forrest still wants revenge against Maggie, she need not worry he'll use her daughter as his means to that end. The angel on his right shoulder has won out over the devil on his left, even though the latter was right that possessing Belinda body and soul would have dealt Maggie the severest blow possible.

Like everybody else who has gotten to know her well, Forrest sees only good in Belinda, and her genuine goodness pulls others to her like a magnet. Everyone she encounters, her father being the prime example, is irresistibly affected by her. And Forrest, a basically decent man, is no exception.

Chapter Twenty-Three

Is Forrest at Long Last Liberated?

Before Forrest can give Olivia the report she deserves, he realizes he must think it through to make sure he fully comprehends what transpired between him and Maggie. A psychologist might recommend he assimilate and analyze everything that was said and seen. Olivia, he knows, would put it more bluntly: "What the hell went on and how do you feel about it?"

Truth was, Forrest was uncertain. That's why he put on his jacket, told Belinda he was heading to his cabin he still rented as a get-away and not to call him unless necessary. "I've got a lot of thinking to do," he told himself, "and I have to do it while everything's still fresh in my memory."

Forrest purchases enough fast food and pop to make leaving the cabin unnecessary, locks the door behind him, grabs some writing paper and a pen, and sits in a comfortable chair by a window. "Got to write down everything we said, everything I saw, and everything running through my mind when Maggie and I were together. Then maybe I can make the best sense of it."

Stopping only to eat and to answer the call of nature, Forrest thinks, writes, and reads for the remainder of the afternoon and most of the evening. He arrives at several conclusions. He no longer feels a need for revenge. He doesn't hate Maggie, nor does he love her. And he feels no desire for her even though she is still a superficially beautiful and sexy woman. What he feels more than anything else, praise God, is *liberated.*

The image he has carried all those years is of a woman who was twenty-one the last time he saw her. That woman he knew and loved so completely no longer exists, just as the man she knew twenty-three years ago is not the same. Time passed them by long ago. Those memories are isolated in another lifetime.

He has no desire to be her friend or to have any kind of a meaningful relationship with her. But he thinks he can be "civil," just as she had said she is willing to be.

"Maybe we can simply leave it at that," he reassures himself.

* * *

The question now is where does all this leave him and Olivia. Does he love her, or is she no more than a sympathetic, fun-to-be-with crutch he has leaned on during his transition period? One thing is certain: He cannot delay finding out because, although she had stated her position more compassionately, she has, in effect, given him an ultimatum. The bigger question is can he be Olivia's lover? That's when they'll both find out if he truly has banished the demons that have haunted him for a quarter of a century.

Mentally exhausted, Forrest promises himself he will call Olivia first thing in the morning and arrange a fateful get-together. Regardless of how things go, it is certain to be memorable. So, it deserves a memorable setting, one any woman would consider ideal. Such a place is nearby: The Greenbrier, West Virginia's world-famous resort in White Sulphur Springs. Forrest lifts the handle of his telephone, puts the call through, reserves the most lavish suite available and orders the royal treatment: champagne, flowers, a horse-drawn carriage ride, sumptuous room-service meals to give them privacy, and a complete spa treatment no woman could refuse.

The date is set.

Chapter Twenty-Four

Anticipation and Anxiety

It's puzzling, Olivia reasons, how a well-educated, worldly attorney who at forty-two has participated in many more of life's experiences than the vast majority of other women could be so nervous about her upcoming rendezvous with Forrest.

On the one hand, she is excited about vacationing at The Greenbrier. Kings and queens, heads of state including twenty-six American presidents, entertainment and sports celebrities, and the wealthy from all over the world have stayed in one of the more than seven hundred guest rooms at the eleven-thousand-acre resort.

All had been pampered and treated royally. They had been massaged, manicured and pedicured, coiffured, exfoliated, waxed, and plucked to a fare-thee-well. They had treated themselves to a dazzling variety of luxury items in the retail shops, eaten the finest cuisine, and had played on the hallowed courses where golf's all-time greats had competed.

But Olivia is nevertheless anxious. What little physical affection that has transpired between her and Forrest has not gone well. His fears of rejection and heartbreak have infected her, making her feel tentative and awkward. She knows how to be romantic, how to make love. She is not a schoolgirl. Problem is, even though she knows what to do, Forrest's reluctance prevents all spontaneity. It is almost as if she needs his permission to participate.

"What an ironic role reversal," she says out loud even though she is alone in her fashionable apartment in downtown Chicago. "That's usually how a man feels—not a woman. No wonder, I seem unprepared. That's never been my worry before."

Yet, she is glad for the opportunity. Forrest has had time to reflect on the "confrontation" Olivia practically ordered him to have with Maggie, and he has promised to be candid in talking with her about it. How did it affect him? What, if anything, changed? Does he still have romantic feelings for Maggie? After more than two decades of being crippled by Maggie, is Forrest finally free of the hold she has had on him all that time? Is he free to love again? To have something approaching a normal romantic sex life?

"A lot is riding on our meeting," she realizes. "I'll come away from it either still with Forrest and having my time at The Greenbrier being a treasured memory, or with Forrest out of my life forever and The Greenbrier being a place I never want to step foot in again.

* * *

Forrest, meanwhile, is having his own agonizing thoughts. His biggest relief is the Maggie of 1987 is not the one he fell in love with in high school. The girl he loved then with all of his being no longer exists. The boy she loved no longer exists either.

His biggest fear is whether this realization means he is capable of "performing" romantic love now that he believes his ties to Maggie have been severed.

With the power his intelligence, his experience, and his great fortune give him, Forrest can control almost everything in his life. But his mind cannot command his body to provide the readiness a male requires to make sexual lovemaking possible. He is so apprehensive, he almost wants to call the whole thing off, but, like Olivia, he would prefer having a loving, compatible life partner than living the lonely alternative.

He has taken every step he can think of to ensure the weekend will be as nearly perfect as is humanly possible. He has sent Olivia a list of every service and activity available at the resort, and the list is dozens of items long. Money is certainly no problem. Nor is time because both he and Olivia have cleared their schedules completely and have left word with all concerned parties they are not to be contacted by any method for any reason "short of World War III."

He will meet her at Yeager Airport in two days.

Chapter Twenty-Five

A Fateful Weekend at The Greenbrier

Olivia's flight is on time, arriving at eleven a.m. She looks radiant
and genuinely happy as Forrest greets her with a warm hug, a light kiss
on the lips, and a genuine smile of his own. He leads her not to his old
Chevy but to a new candy apple red Jaguar sedan. Olivia's mouth forms a
startled "O" at her first sight of it, and Forrest bursts out laughing,
reminding her he had warned her previously his tastes stop just short of
gaudy.

"I toned it down inside," he points out as if to make amends. "See,
it's all in white."

"Well, if we attract any whistles while were in this thing, I'll know
it's the car and not me," she concedes.

"I'm hungry, Forrest. Charleston's big enough to be full of good res-
taurants. Want to eat here?"

"Nope. I have another place in mind if you can hold off a couple of
hours."

"It better be good because my stomach's already growling."

"I think you'll find it is, Olivia. I haven't been there since my family
used to take me after we visited the state fair nearby. It's a really historic
place called The General Lewis Inn, located in an authentically historic
little town called Lewisburg, just before we get to The Greenbrier in
White Sulphur Springs."

"Fine. But get me a couple of candy bars to tide me over."

"Will do."

* * *

Once again Forrest avoids the interstate after leaving it at Beckley and drives through Daniels, takes WV 3 East through Jumping Branch and on to Hinton. It's a pretty drive, but that's not his main reason for going that way. He wants Olivia to experience what has to be nineteen miles down one of the most twisting, turning, edge-of-the-mountain drives in North America. Until she had seen the overlook at Grandview State Park, Olivia had bemoaned the fact that she didn't feel as if she were traveling in the mountains. Forrest is willing to bet she'll never bring that up again.

"Good grief, Forrest. You should have warned me. I would have taken a Dramamine. You're damned lucky I didn't throw up all over your brand new white upholstery."

"It served my purpose," he jokes.

"What do you mean?"

"I think it cured your hunger."

"Well, think again. I'll get even by ordering the most expensive meals on the menu in Lewisburg and in White Sulphur Springs. Please tell me the rest of the road there isn't as bad."

"No," Forrest assures her. "I think you've had the ultimate hilly experience, so we'll get on I-64 near Hinton. It'll take us everywhere else we want to go."

While Forrest enjoys being behind the wheel of his sporty, powerful, smooth-driving Jag, Olivia takes in the scenery of one of the most beautiful areas in the state. Lots of farm country, plenty of animals, and mile after mile of evergreen and deciduous trees and shrubs that appear rich and green, invigorated by the generous annual rainfall of about forty inches, and only a few buildings anywhere more than three stories high.

Quite a contrast to Chicago where she has lived all her life except for college in the East. She takes it in with the wide-eyed curiosity of a child.

Forrest turns onto Exit 169, drives Oliva by the quaint houses lining the streets of historic Lewisburg before heading for the General Lewis Inn. It is an all-white building, parts of which date back to 1834. It sits on a knoll and features five tall, white columns. It is not large, having fewer than thirty guest rooms, but it radiates old world charm balanced with comfortable amenities.

Olivia unabashedly gawks at every detail, focusing on a fascinating display of antique farm implements as Forrest steers her toward a table by a window.

"Got your appetite back yet?" he teases.

"Oh, yeah. The waiter better bring two pens to write down my order. Forrest closes his menu in less than a minute, but Olivia reads every choice. "You made up your mind fast, Forrest. What are you having?"

"A good old West Virginia meal called Redneck Benedict."

"And what's that?" Olivia says with a sour look. "Eggs with chicken feathers still on them?"

"Not quite. Fried eggs, country ham, buttermilk biscuits, sausage gravy, and grits."

"Well, enjoy your trip down Hillbilly Memory Lane, and don't bother explaining what grits are. I don't want to spoil my appetite."

Olivia orders a steak, cooked as rare as the law allows, and adds a Caesar salad and asparagus tips.

Neither has dessert. They are already anticipating a fabulous evening meal.

* * *

The Greenbrier lives up to its reputation. The entrance is long enough for Olivia to get a look at the huge white building in all of its glory. The gardeners and groundskeepers have placed a variety of colorful flower beds strategically along the manicured lawn. To a first-time visitor like Olivia, the sight is entrancing.

Before they go to their suite, Forrest has their luggage taken care of and leads Olivia by the hand toward the retail shops, stopping at a window displaying a dazzling collection of necklaces, bracelets, and rings. She suspects nothing, but Forrest has conspired with her mother and sister and has a surprise in store.

They enter and Forrest introduces himself and Olivia to an associate offering assistance. He is expected. The manager is alerted, and she and the associate display a breathtakingly beautiful, one-of-a-kind, cushion-set diamond and emerald cocktail ring in eighteen carat white gold. The emerald is surrounded by round brilliant diamonds spaced evenly between eight smaller, round emeralds. It is Olivia's favorite gemstone, according to her mother and sister, who also know Olivia's ring size.

It's a perfect fit, as Forrest knew it would be, and Olivia realizes instantly that is too much of a coincidence. Unless custom ordered, rings have to be sized.

"Forrrrreeeessst?" she accuses in a sing-song, drawn-out tone.

"Yep, it's yours. Just my way of saying thanks for all you've done, all your visits, and all your wonderful ideas and help in bringing Old Mrs. Kimble's mansion back to life."

"Forrest, you know I shouldn't . . . ."

"But you will, won't you?"

"Oh, hell yes. If you were pursuing me, I might feel compromised. But because it's the other way around, I'll consider this a keepsake . . . with the emphasis on 'keep'. Thank you, thank you, thank you," she says sincerely and kisses Forrest fully on the lips in front of everyone in the store, some of whom stare and smile while the employees applaud.

"Now what are you going to do to top this?" she teases.

"I don't think I can. But before we go to our suite and order dinner, we're going to take a carriage ride around the grounds and let a handsome horse do the driving."

* * *

After a refreshing shower for Forrest and a long, warm soaking bath for Olivia, they have coffee and dessert freshly made and delivered to their suite.

"Oooooooh," Olivia almost yawns with an expression of deep satisfaction. "Thank you for a perfect day, Forrest. I enjoyed the drive, the surprise visit to that charming old General Lewis Inn, and everything— simply everything—about The Greenbrier, especially this gorgeous ring I may never remove from my finger."

As she closes her eyes and leans back in her chair, feeling blissfully relaxed and allowing herself to fully enjoy the moment, Forrest takes a long, appreciative look at her. Olivia is so unlike the Maggie of his youth.

Where Maggie was flamboyant, full-figured and stunningly sexy, Olivia is more of an elegant, dignified, classic beauty. They are both tall, but Olivia is much smaller. She is not skinny, Forrest is pleased to note. He thinks women whose rib, chest, and shoulder bones are too prominent look like underdeveloped adolescent boys. Olivia's body, though not voluptuous like Maggie's, is nonetheless perfectly proportioned and thoroughly feminine. Even her delicate hands are exquisite.

The word that best describes Olivia as a whole, Forrest concludes, is refined. Her thick bluish-black hair, milky-white skin, and gray eyes are a rare combination. To Forrest, she looks much like a porcelain doll, reflecting her Russian heritage. Her family, part of the minor nobility, escaped to the United States during the revolution of 1917 when the Bolsheviks overthrew the Imperial Government and ended the Romanov's three-hundred-year dynasty. Olivia's forebears were more fortunate than most, managing to get away with the family jewels, which they invested in business ventures and prospered.

His "examination" is interrupted as Olivia's rest ends with an invitation: "Join me on the sofa?"

"Love to."

To Forrest, this day with Olivia is strangely reminiscent of Senior Prom night with Maggie. He approached each with hopeful anticipation of finally experiencing something elusive and yet wonderful. He had longed throughout his high school years for the opportunity to make love for the first time in his life. And he wanted that experience to be with Maggie. Now that he believes he is free of her, he longs equally to have romantic love again, for the first time since Maggie. This time with Olivia.

And he is determined that it, too, will be a memory of a lifetime. He pledges to himself that he will take all the time in the world, forbidding his passion from hastening past all the tender touching and caressing she and all other women deserve to be assured they are loved romantically and thoroughly.

Forrest positions himself behind Olivia on the sofa, circles her waist with his arms, and pulls her back against him, gently rubbing her shoulders with his strong hands. She responds with encouraging low moans that increase in intensity as Forrest adds a shower of brief, wet kisses to her neck, back and upper arms.

With neither saying a word, he unbuttons her blouse, all the while rubbing and kissing lower, eventually removing the upper garment and leaving Olivia naked from the waist up except for her bra, which he has not touched.

He guides her gently forward into a reclining position face down and caresses her from her waist to her shapely thighs and calves. Her body is extraordinary, and he is becoming as excited as he is making her.

He takes her softly under her shoulders and pulls her up again, positioning his hands until both touch her navel. He inches them up to her breasts, cupping the outside of her bra before releasing the clasps in back and removing it. He breathes in sharply as he returns to her exposed breasts and rubs his palms over them.

Eager to move to the next level, Olivia rolls onto her back, unzips her skirt and maneuvers it to the floor. She has only one article of apparel remaining, but Forrest is still fully clothed. She takes her turn, unbuttoning his shirt and returning the pleasure he has given her, massaging and kissing his face, neck, and chest.

Forrest moves between her legs without lowering his body on hers, covering every square inch of her front with kisses and caresses from neck to ankle, pausing just long enough to remove his trousers. Breathing heavily and rapidly, Forrest and Olivia have reached the point of no return. Both are mindful that Forrest has neither hesitated nor backed away.

"I'll just die if he quits now," Olivia agonizes. "I must know," she determines, aggressively pulling his body down on hers. To her delight and relief, Forrest's readiness is unmistakable. As he gets totally nude, she accepts that as a signal and does likewise.

Finally, they join, releasing the fire of desire they have been stoking for a frustratingly long time. They exchange hot, penetrating kisses and meet each other's movements with the timing of experienced lovers until they burst into a climax of utter ecstasy.

Chapter Twenty-Six

The Mansion's "Coming Out Party"

Both Olivia and Belinda take for granted Forrest will plan a black-tie gala as the first event to show off his magnificent mansion after spending millions of dollars over the year and a half it took to reinforce, restore, and redecorate it.

But they are wrong.

"We're not social climbers trying to impress the local gentry," he reminds them as they enjoy a snack in his back-to-the-fifties basement. "I want to invite the people who had a big part in turning my dream house into a reality."

"Like who, Forrest?" Olivia asks. "Even this huge place can't accommodate everybody who pounded a nail or painted a wall."

"I've thought about that," Forrest replies. "I'm going to invite the local business owners who provided the materials, and the foremen and bosses for every crew that did a substantial part of the work—electrical, structural, plumbing, painting, and so forth. And, of course, their spouses."

"Is that it?" Belinda jumps in when Forrest pauses for breath. She has a list of her own. "What about the lawyers, John and Cassandra? Barney and Calvin who did the inspection and evaluation? The architects, the interior decorators? The artists who created the paintings and stained glass? And Louisa and Alistair Malcolmson?"

"And, Forrest, I just thought about your basketball-playing buddies. Surely, they will be coming," Olivia chimes in.

"Way ahead of you both. Thank you all the same. I've included all of them with Louisa and Alistair being the guests of honor. However, I'm saving my boyhood buddies and their families for a special time that I've already given them a date for. I have a big surprise planned for them, but it's not ready yet. As far as any other potential guests are concerned, I'll give you a list, and you can add others if you want. OK?"

They both nod yes.

"Will your parents be coming, and your brother and sister and their families?" Belinda asks, her mind still busily ticking off anyone else who should be on Forrest's list.

"No, they're coming for Thanksgiving. Mother and dad feel uncomfortable stuck in a room full of strangers. You may invite your folks then, too, if you want."

"My mother!" Belinda laughs. "You better give that a little more thought, don't you think?"

Forrest just smiles, but Olivia is relieved she doesn't have to face being in the same room with Maggie for at least a few more months. Olivia quickly changes the subject. What about the date, the menu, the caterer, people to serve, to park cars, and all that?"

"That's why The Good Lord put the two of you in my life," Forrest says with a sly look and a wink. "I'm putting Belinda in charge. She knows all the local people we need to hire, and, Olivia, you can coordinate with Belinda from Chicago."

"I presume you want to keep things simple then?" Olivia says as she begins to take notes."

"Yes. Meat loaf, fried chicken, catfish—that sort of thing. A good wine but no liquor. Plain dress. They can wear blue jeans for all I care."

"Oh, no," Olivia objects. "I might defer to you on most things, Forrest, but I have to put my foot down on such informal dress. Believe me —and Belinda will back me up a hundred percent—you cannot deprive the women a chance to dress up, get their hair and makeup done, and wear their best jewelry. All the people on your list can afford all that. Dress should at the very least be church suitable."

"Olivia is right, Forrest," Belinda emphasizes.

"Fine with me. You're handling the invitations, too. Do anything and everything you want; I'll take care of my part."

"And what exactly is that?" Olivia asks suspiciously.

"Paying the bills and enjoying myself. What else? The rest I leave in your very capable hands, ladies."

Chapter Twenty-Seven

What the Party-Goers Experience

Over the next three weeks, Belinda and Olivia make all necessary preparations for the mansion's "Coming Out Party," following Forrest's instructions to the letter.

Well, almost.

Meatloaf, chicken, and catfish have been replaced on the menu by filet mignon and almond-crusted salmon. Dessert will be delayed until after the grand tour and will consist of banana splits and milkshakes served in the back-to-the-fifties soda shop. Dancing will follow for those so inclined with music provided by the period-correct Wurlitzer juke box. Forrest makes clear anyone attempting to "do the twist" will be immediately ejected and forever banned from the mansion.

* * *

Instead of turning off McDowell Road and parking on the east side of the house as Forrest, Belinda, and frequent guests do, those invited to the party enter from the front and are given the full hospitality treatment. What they see as they turn off Rhododendron Ridge is the multi-patterned brick driveway, illuminated by antique lampposts and wide enough to accommodate two lanes of cars parked side by side.

Gleaming white bricks, painstakingly scrubbed clean from almost a century of accumulated dirt and grime, are accentuated by long black shutters on every window. They are topped by a new slate shingle roof in a mixture of green, white, and black.

Wide stone steps take guests to the fifteen-foot-wide wrap-around porch and on to the giant oak double doors. Forrest and Olivia greet each couple and Belinda escorts them into the Great Room where they are served Dom Perignon champagne and hot and cold hors d'oeuvres. The meal will follow at eight o'clock in the Dining Hall.

The Chicago interior designers, working in conjunction with Oliva and Belinda, have decorated the main and second floors as authentically as possible with Victorian Era furniture, draperies, rugs and carpets, hand-blown glass, and other *objets d'art*. The rooms are completed in the best of taste and do not even begin to challenge Forrest's penchant for stopping "one step short of gaudy."

Victorian era furniture is far more beautiful than it is comfortable, but Forrest has little personal use for the formal rooms except for parties and receptions. The dark, heavy wood is embellished with carvings of vines, leaves and fruits across the tops of the couches and chairs, and rose and cranberry velvet have been chosen as the material for seats and backs. Forrest would describe the couches as being "scalloped" shaped.

Most of the tables have thick marble tops, and the vases and other decorative objects are mostly yellow, cranberry, and cobalt blue. Several are adorned with hand-painted flowers or formally dressed adults, children, and pets. The heavy draperies are multi-layered with lace curtains.

Forrest took an active part only in the selection of paintings. He knows very little about art or art history, but like almost everybody else he knows what he likes when he sees it. And what he likes are the paintings of the impressionists, especially Monet and Renior. He approves of their choice of ordinary subject matter, their use of varying shades of light, and their emphasis on impression over details.

In trying to express his admiration of the impressionists, Forrest told the Chicago decorators he very much likes what seems to him to be "a dreamy, fading image of pleasant memories passing into time."

To illustrate the feeling he was trying to get across to them, Forrest made the following fine reproduction choices, among others: Monet's "Nympheas" (water lilies) and "Impression, sunrise"; Renoir's "Two Young Girls at the Piano" and "Bal du Moulin de la Galette" showing happy people dancing; "Dinner at the Ball" and "Woman Combing Her Hair" by Degas; Toulouse-Lautrec's "At the Moulin Rouge'; Gassatt's "Summertime"; "Bar at the Folles-Bergere" by Manet; Morisot's "Young Woman at her Looking Glass"; and "Irises" by Van Gogh.

Bedrooms with canopy beds and ornate dressers follow the Victorian theme on the second floor, and each opens into a large sitting room. A balcony crosses the front of the entire floor.

The ladies presented all designs and purchases to Forrest for payment and purposely avoided asking for his approval. He told Olivia he would give her free rein over everything above his beloved fifties-era basement, except for his library and the meditation room/chapel. And he kept his word.

He did feel confident enough in his knowledge of things Appalachian to guide Olivia in her selections for the attic, which, like the fifties-theme basement, is a startling departure in design from the first two floors. Truth be told, neither the basement nor the attic look as if they were intended to be placed in anybody's grand mansion. But they thoroughly please Forrest.

Anyone walking up the newly constructed steps from the twelve-foot-tall second story to the seven-foot-high attic would enter an entirely different world filled with barnwood floors and walls, log furniture, genuine mountain rifles, wood carvings, Appalachian arts collected at fairs and antique shops, handmade quilts and baskets, paintings honoring Forrest's coal-mining forebears and numerous historical events, hand thrown pottery—just anything and everything that struck Forrest's and

Olivia's fancy. Daniel Boone probably would have felt very much at home in such a setting.

* * *

At dinner, Belinda offers a prayer of thanksgiving for the wondrously restored and decorated mansion, for the talent and contributions of one and all present, and to Forrest, who dedicated a quarter of a century of work and planning toward making his dream come true. She ends by asking God to enlighten Forrest to find ways to share his home, and especially its inspirational chapel, with as many others as possible.

Surprisingly, Barney Summerfield, who did not strike Forrest as a willing public speaker, asks for the privilege of offering a toast.

"Keep your seats, folks. Forrest said tonight was gonna be informal, so we can lift our glasses just as well without standin'. I just wanna remind Forrest of what I said when he and Calvin Quesenberry—seated to my left here—and I left this place after our preliminary inspection. I said I felt sad down deep in my soul for Old Mrs. Kimble's mansion because if it had feelin's, it wudda been embarrassed about how bad of a shape it was in.

"Well, when my wife, Bernice, and I turned up the driveway a little while ago, I took one look and got a lump as big as this mansion in my throat. As a builder, I love nothing more than seein' a good work of restoration completed. But there's nothin' in my experience that compares—or ever will come close to comparin'—with what magnificent work has been done on this mansion. So, congratulations, Forrest. Here's wishing yuh many years of good health and wonderful times in yer dream home."

As the cheers die down, Forrest stands, and encouraging everyone to eat as he speaks, he thanks them for coming. "Thank all of you for all that you and your employees did. Thanks also, of course, to Olivia and Belinda, who did not only their part but also most of mine. We welcome our guests of honor, Louisa and Alistair Malcolmson, and special thanks also go to John Vermillion and Cassandra Pierce, our lawyer friends who made the purchase without revealing my name and have also kept everything nice and legal as we've moved along.

"I've already expressed my gratitude to each of you in individual letters because I am so pleased and happy with how things turned out I wanted to put it in writing and on the record. Please know that if the letter or any further recommendation from me can be of help in promoting your businesses, you certainly have my permission.

"After we finish dinner, we'll take a leisurely tour, and I want each of you to talk about and point out what you or your company did. And do not be modest. We can all brag a little tonight. We'll start with the first two floors, move to the attic, and finish in the basement—which, by the way, I'm going to quit calling a basement because it really is a fifties-era diner with a dance floor.

"We have our architect, Margaret Tutwiler, here, and our Chicago designers, Christina Merryweather and Patrick O'Donnell, as well as Katherine Montgomery and Anton Borislaw, who not only designed and supervised the creation of our stained glass but also did some of the most delicate work themselves. The artists who painted the West Virginia scenes in the library are also here: Lydell Hendrickson, Vanessa Jefferson, and Winston Tarrington.

"I look forward to your comments as we walk through the rooms."

* * *

An hour and a half later, everyone gathers in the "diner" to enjoy dessert. At Forrest's urging, several couples go over to the jukebox and make selections of rock 'n roll songs they jitterbugged to back when. Some evidently have not danced in a while and are a little off their timing, but Forrest appreciates their efforts all the same.

What really surprises him though is discovering the best dancers by far are Barney and Bernice. "Damn!" Forrest exclaims out loud. "They're better than Maggie and I ever were, despite the extra fifty pounds neither probably had when they were in high school." Forrest makes a mental note to put Barney and Bernice on his "must invite list" for all appropriate occasions.

"Want to join in?" Olivia and Belinda ask Forrest almost simultaneously.

"You know how to do this dance, Belinda? It died out a few years after you were born, you know."

"No problem," she replies. "At least in this one respect, I am my mother's daughter."

"That settles it then," Forrest grins. "I'll dance with both of you at the same time. I danced double a lot in my younger days, and I don't mind showing off my skills to an appreciative audience. Olivia, take my left hand with your right, and, Belinda, take my right hand with your right, and just follow my lead."

After a little confusion and bumping into one another, Forrest solves the under-the-arm twirling and ends the dance between the women with one arm around each of their waists, doing fancy steps forward and backward in perfect time to the music. Dancing goes on for another hour.

An appropriate conclusion to a memorable evening.

* * *

However, across town at the New River Golf and Country Club, things are not going so well for Maggie and Nat Buckingham. Maggie had been in a gloomy mood all day, sulking about missing out on the big doings at the Kimble mansion. She fully understood why Belinda was on the invitation list and she was not. But Maggie has never budged from being at the center of her own universe, and being rational about things she is justifiably denied is not the way her mind works.

Nat, as usual, was burdened with "fixing" her. He wanted to stay home and watch television, but Maggie would be hell to live with the entire weekend if she couldn't have a good time, just like everybody at Forrest's party.

"Maggie, honey," he says barely above a whisper as he figuratively sticks in his toe to test the troubled waters. "How about us getting all dressed up and having dinner at the country club? They'll have a band there tonight and there will be dancing." By invoking that magic word, Nat succeeds in putting color back into Maggie's cheeks.

"I'll be ready in one hour," she promises. "Wear some comfortable shoes because I'm not going to miss out on a single dance."

And Maggie does not. Fortunately for Nat, several of his golfing buddies and their wives are present, and they all enjoy dancing with beautiful Maggie, who still can move with all of the skills she had in high school.

Maggie not only matches her partners dance for dance but also drink for drink, which causes her to be loud and to add too many risqué moves while dancing with the husbands of other women. The wives do not like it and neither does Nat, who consoles himself by downing one drink after another.

By the end of the evening, both Nat and Maggie are obviously too drunk to drive themselves home, so their sober friends, Darnell and Nancy Shumate, deliver them and their car safely to their doorstep.

Chapter Twenty-Eight

Maggie's World Falls Apart

Ten hours after they leave the party, Nat is in the county morgue with a six-inch knife wound in his chest, and a badly hungover Maggie is in the city jail charged with murder.

By noon everybody who is answering the phone has gotten the word, and after friends and acquaintances recover from the numbing shock, speculation spreads like a wildfire. It has never been a secret that Maggie and Nat had more of an arrangement than a marriage, and many of Nat's friends had often served as sounding boards for his complaints about Maggie's frigidness after the birth of their son.

As far as many of the locals are concerned, Maggie is guilty before she has her arraignment. "All she ever wanted was the Buckingham name and their money," is the consensus. And they are right; that is all she wanted from Nat, other than his acquiescence.

When completely sober, Maggie would be much too wise to answer probing questions by police detectives without her lawyer present. But at the time of her arrest, she had not gotten all of the alcohol out of her system, and she talks far more than she should.

She tells lead Detective Chester Foy she remembers nothing between the time she went to bed and when she got up about six thirty to go to the kitchen for some water and found her husband's fully clothed, blood-smeared body lying face up on the couch. "That's as far as he made it after we came through the front door last night," she explains.

And, no, neither she nor Nat set the alarm. "It was all we could do just to get to a bed."

And, no, she could not account for the blood on her hands, her night clothes, and her bed covers. "If I left my bed before six thirty, I have no memory of it."

And, yes, she does recognize the knife. "It's from a set we keep in the kitchen."

And, no, they had not been quarreling. "We had a fine time at the country club. Both of us were in a good mood."

And, no, she did not kill her husband. That question proves sobering enough to alert Maggie to declare, "I'm saying nothing more until my lawyer is present."

Detective Foy did not get to ask Maggie what she stood to gain financially from her husband's death, but during his investigation over the next several days, he discovers it is a great deal. Maggie stands to share ten million dollars in life insurance with the two children, Belinda and Nat V. Stocks, bonds, and cash amounting to another eighteen million also would be split three ways. Maggie alone would inherit the house and furnishings worth about four million.

"In my seventeen years on the force, I've arrested a bunch of people who have killed for a few hundred dollars," Foy tells Adam Zeller, the prosecutor. "I can't even imagine the number of people who would commit murder for what Mrs. Buckingham will get her hands on if we don't convict her."

"I'm pretty confident I can do that," Zeller says. "We have motive, an unstable marriage, a shit pot full of money, and plenty of circumstantial evidence at this point."

Zeller not only is confident, he is practically salivating at the chance to enhance his reputation by winning a scandalous murder trial involving a prominent, wealthy family. There will be maximum media coverage, and like many other ambitious prosecutors, he thinks Adam Zeller would sound a whole lot grander with "Governor" in front of it.

* * *

Maggie's lawyer, Augustus Alouishus McDermott, arrives at police headquarters within a half hour of her call. Like everybody else, Maggie calls him Gus, to the everlasting consternation of his mother. who failed to anticipate the snooty name she so carefully selected would be reduced by classmates to a one-syllable grunt answered to by many, but by none among the blue bloods.

Gus, who much prefers his nickname over that god-awful pretentious appellation on his birth certificate, nevertheless made his mother proud by graduating in the top ten percent of his law class at West Virginia University. And because of his street-fighter tactics and his creativity in concocting "evidence" to raise reasonable doubt in the minds of jurors, he is one of the most sought-after and highly paid criminal attorneys in the state.

"Don't worry," Gus assures the haggard Maggie, looking conspicuously unfashionable in her ill-fitting bright orange jail uniform. "I'll have you back in your house in time for dinner. Listen to me carefully and remember my words. What fingerprints there were on the knife were so badly smudged, they are unidentifiable. I'm sure the blood on your hands and on your nightgown resulted from your holding your beloved husband in your arms after you checked his pulse and confirmed he was dead. And the blood got on your bed because that's where you collapsed from grief after using the phone on the nightstand to dial 911. Isn't that the way you remember it, Maggie?"

"Oh, oh yeah, Gus. That's, that's exactly the way I remember it."

"Is that the way you explained it to Detective Foy?"

"I don't think so. I think I told him I didn't remember anything between going to bed and finding Nat's body early this morning."

"That's OK, Maggie. That's perfectly understandable. It's clear to me you were too distraught to think rationally. But now, upon reflection, it happened as I explained. Correct?"

"Damn right, Gus. Precisely."

"All right. Hang tight. I'm going to have a talk with Foy, the police chief, and the assistant district attorney and see about getting you home."

"Thanks, Gus. You're a marvel."

"I'll remind you about that when I send you my bill," Gus grins as he leaves the room.

* * *

"You don't have sufficient evidence to charge my client," Gus states unflinchingly to Foy, Chief Mark Crowe, and Assistant DA Florence Berlin. "You don't have her fingerprints on the knife, and my explanation for the blood on her hands, clothing, and bed sheets is so logical, no judge could deny the possibility or even the probability."

"Gus, you know damn good and well she killed Nat as sure as Cain murdered Abel—guilty just like virtually all your other clients," Foy spits back, seething with disgust.

"Sticks and stones, detective. Sticks and stones," Gus responds with a practiced smirk that Foy would dearly love to smack off his face.

"All right, Mr. McDermott, we'll release her as soon as we can process her," Chief Crowe concedes after consulting with Berlin. "But I agree with Chester. She's guilty as hell, and it won't be long before she's back in jail where she belongs."

"I'll walk you to your car, Gus," Foy insists. "Which one did you drive today?" he asks tauntingly. "The Mercedes sedan? "The Volvo station wagon? Or your little midlife crisis '57 T-Bird?"

"The T-Bird, Foy. I was feeling kinda sporty this morning. Like to sit in it, would you?"

"Hell-ul no! But if I did have a car like that, I could sit in it without a guilty conscience over how I earned the money to buy it. Tell me, Gus, does your mother realize her favorite son pays for his cars, his big house, his country club membership, his fancy clothes, and his kids' private school with money raked in for twisting the truth to get criminals off so they can return to the streets and cheat, rob, and kill more innocent people?"

"Sticks and stones, Foy. Sticks and stones. Oh, and by the way, does your mother know how you cops always pick the easiest suspect, select only the evidence that helps and hide the rest, and sleep soundly at night knowing jails and prisons are full of innocent people you helped send there?"

"Kiss my ass, Gus."

"Pucker up yourself, detective."

Chapter Twenty-Nine

LeRoy Bares His Soul to Belinda

Belinda and LeRoy have seen each other frequently since he told her of his terminal illness, finally getting acquainted firsthand instead of gleaning bits and pieces of information from others as they have done since she was born. Other than losing his hair and some weight, he had been functioning remarkably well after recovering from his chemotherapy and radiation treatments.

But all of that has changed in the past week after a series of minor strokes was followed by a major one that left LeRoy paralyzed on his right side. Belinda spends as much time with him as she can. Fortunately, his mind is intact, and his speech is good enough to be understood.

Belinda believes everything is part of God's comprehensive plan for each person's life, and she is determined to heed His call to save her father's soul. She has learned over the years not to be too "preachy." That has cost her a couple of friends who liked their lifestyle and didn't want it spoiled even the least little bit by an evangelizing Belinda. But her dad— that was a different matter altogether. He was dying; time was precious.

"Tell me what you've learned since I gave you your assignment, Dad. You have been reading your Bible, following the outline I typed for you?"

"I have indeed, Belinda. I read again the parable 'bout thuh prodigal son. Yuh told me I didn't git the proper meanin' when I said I thought that boy deserved tuh be punished instead of treated like a returnin' hero and such, 'specially when yuh thank about how overlooked it made his brother feel 'cause he had stayed at home and worked hard fer his father.

"Well, I talked it over with Aunt Willa, and she said fer me to thank of God bein' the father and the boy a sinner who had rebelled against him. So what I got outta it the second time is the boy stood fer sinners like me, and the father was God showin' that no matter how bad a life a body has lived, God's always ready tuh forgive him and welcome him back into His family. Sound 'bout right tuh yuh?"

Tears of confirmation make a path down Belinda's cheeks, her big smile diverting them toward the back of her face. "Oh, Dad, I am so pleased. Praise God and praise you. Now do you fully understand that no matter how you have lived and no matter what you have done, it's not too late for you to be saved?"

"Well, I don't understand how God can be that fergivin', so I'll just have tuh accept it on faith. Butcha must understand, He knows horrible thangs 'bout me that I never wanna tell yuh."

"You don't have to tell me, or anyone else for that matter. Just so you confess it to Him. That's all you have to do other than to be sincere. You can be at peace about that. I promise."

"OK then, Belinda. But tuh do what yuh've been leadin' me tuh do all these weeks we been meetin' means I'll have tuh make one confession publicly, and it'll cause a real ruckus in this town. It'll be in all the papers and on radio and TV, and the gossips 'round here will have a high ol' time talkin' 'bout it.

"Worst of all, it'll bring hurt tuh yuh. When yuh learn 'bout it, I thank yuh'll agree I'm doin' thuh right thang in makin' it known, but it'll hurt yuh terrible all the same. Yuh sure yuh want bad enough fer me tuh get right with God tuh take thuh consequences?"

"I don't know what you've done to justify the fallout you just described, Dad. But God will help me and everybody else get through it."

"Yuh won't turn against me and hate me, then, Belinda? I couldn't bear dyin' with yuh hatin' me."

"I will stick by you no matter what, Dad. As God is my witness."

"Then send the police chief or one of his detectives tuh see me. And yuh better make it soon 'cause I don't think I'm gonna be 'round much longer."

Chapter Thirty

LeRoy's Confession Causes a Ruckus

"All right, Mr. Bottoms. We are all here at the request of your daughter, Belinda. I'm Chief Mark Crowe, and the three others are Detective Chester Foy, Assistant District Attorney Florence Berlin, and Hugh Mounts who will record everything we say. Belinda said you had something to confess that concerns our community. Of course, we want to know what that is. So, please, tell us everything, and start with the reason you are voluntarily making a confession."

"Well, chief, it's 'cause my daughter wants my eternal soul saved 'fore I die, and I could go at any time. I got stage four lung cancer, and it's spread everwhur, and now these strokes . . . I done a lotta thangs wrong durin' my life, and I'd prefer goin' tuh my grave without lettin' on I done any of 'em. But Belinda's a strong believer and tells me I have tuh confess everthang tuh git right with the Lord.

"She said I don't have tuh tell nobody 'cept God, and that's what I done. But the one I'm gonna tell about today has tuh be set right publicly 'cause if I don't, somebody else is gonna be blamed. And God wouldn't approve of that, and neither would Belinda. 'Til just a few weeks ago, I've been a crappy dad, so I'm damn sure not gonna disappoint her again.

"Yuh see, what I done was I kilt a man, right here in Asher Heights. Nat Buckingham, my ex-wife's husband and Belinda's stepfather." LeRoy pauses to let his revelation sink in, observing the genuine surprise on the faces of the public officials, whom he obviously has caught totally off guard.

Belinda has trouble catching her breath. Hearing LeRoy confess to committing murder is horrifying enough. Hearing the victim was her stepfather, a man she loved dearly for treating her as if she were his own flesh and blood, produces an overwhelming conflict. She immediately prays silently.

"Lord, I am deeply grateful you have used me as your instrument for having my father save his soul by making this public confession. But please, God, help me to reconcile all of this and find peace. I give this burden to you, Dear Father, because it's more than I can endure."

"Go on, Mr. Bottoms," the chief encourages, getting everyone's attention again, including Belinda's. "Tell us why you did it, how you did it, and who all else, if anybody, was involved."

"Just me. Nobody else. I know y'all figger Maggie done it or got somebody tuh do it fer her. But she didn't. I done it alone, and that's thuh God's truth of it.

"Maggie don't have no use fer me at all since our divorce all those years ago. I broke up her engagement tuh a much better man just tuh prove tuh myself I could. She was beautiful, and I wanted her tuh be with me 'til I got tired of her. That's the way I treated all women back then. I know yuh won't believe it tuh look at me now, but I was handsome and built real good back then. I had all kinds of women.

"Why did I do it? Fer money. What else? That's why I've always broke thuh law. Money fer booze, money fer drugs, money so I wouldn't have tuh work steady."

"But how would killing Mr. Buckingham put money in your pocket unless Mrs. Buckingham or someone else paid you to do it?" Foy asked.

" 'Cause I knew Belinda would be left millions, seein' as how Mr. Buckingham looked upon her like she was his own kin. And 'cause she's such a righteous person, I coulda told her a bunch of lies so she'd gimme some of it before the cancer kilt me. But as I said, I wasn't much of a dad, but she loved me anyhow. Gittin' money from her wudda been easy. I didn't thank I'd be dyin' so soon.' "

The officers watch as what is left of LeRoy's shriveled, diseased body shakes with sorrow, tears of remorse streaming down his face.

"Mr. Bottoms," Chief Crowe says quietly when LeRoy is able to speak again, "we need to confirm one more thing and then we'll let you rest for a while. How did you kill Nat Buckingham?"

LeRoy looks the chief in the eye and says without emotion, "With a knife I took from his and Maggie's kitchen. I'd been watchin' their movements fer a couple of weeks, tryin' tuh git a good time tuh catch him alone and off guard. But they gotta first-class security system, and they always lock thur doors. That night, when I seen others bringin' 'em home after some big party, it was plain both Maggie and Nat was so drunk, they needed help walkin'.

"I figgered if they was ever gonna be careless, this was it. And I was right. Not only didn't they turn on their alarm, they didn't even lock their front door. I sneaked in quiet like, seen Mr. Buckingham passed out on the couch, and clothes Maggie must of left goin' up thuh staircase. I figgered she was undressin' as she went and would be out cold on her bed as well.

"Anyhow, I stood outta sight and listened fer a spell. And when I was sure they wasn't conscious, I walked into thuh kitchen, found the knife, and stabbed Mr. Buckingham through thuh heart. He never made a sound; never knew he'd been kilt. Then 'stead of wipin' my fingerprints off the knife, I smudged 'em so it wouldn't look so deliberate. I made sure I didn't leave no fingerprints anywhurs else and just walked away.

"Now, if yuh don't mind, I'm wore out. If yuh'll go, I'll tell yuh later anythang else yuh wanna know. Just one favor, please. Gimme a week tuh die here in Aunt Wilma's house. If I last longer than that, then yuh can take me tuh jail."

***

LeRoy's prediction that the news would cause a ruckus in the town turned out to be an understatement. Phones rang off the hook; a special edition flew off the newspaper's presses; and radio and television reporters interrupted regular programs four or five times an hour with "special reports," even when all they did was repeat what everyone had already known for hours.

Reactions of the townspeople were split. Some were relieved for Maggie; others were firm in their conviction that "she was behind it all and was getting off free as you please."

The mayor was happy not to have a long, drawn out trial. "Bad for business," he insisted.

Chief Crowe was glad to get the pressure off his back by having the case solved.

Detective Foy was mad as hell that he couldn't somehow tie Maggie to the killing and see that "sorry son of a bitch Gus McDermott get his ass kicked in a public trial."

When would-be governor Adam Zeller was informed of the confession, he stomped out of his office, went home and had the male equivalent of a hissy fit in front of his introverted but relieved wife, who had no desire to lose all of her privacy by becoming the state's first lady.

Belinda prays some significant "good news" event will quickly come along to snatch the public's attention and point it in another direction.

She does not get her wish. Nat's parents and siblings see to that, at least for a time, backed by their formidable influence and great fortune.

***

No one is dismayed more by LeRoy's confession than Nat's family. They despise the very air Maggie breathes and believe a guilty verdict would put her out of their lives for good. They are steadfast in their belief from the beginning of their son's pursuit of Maggie that her only interest in him was his family's revered name and its large fortune. They hate the thought of her inheriting millions of dollars belonging to their loved one she had purposely misused and then for all practical purposes discarded like an empty wine bottle.

However, the Buckingham family faces a dilemma. They not only dearly love Nat's son, but they also love Belinda as much as they loathe her mother. "She's as close to being an angel on earth as a person can get," Mrs. Buckingham had stated publicly on numerous occasions. "Not a deceitful bone in her body, and sweet and loving as they come. I love her as much as I do any of my biological grandchildren." Her husband, their children, and their other grandchildren all shared Mrs. Buckingham's feelings for Belinda.

"God help us, she loves her mother," Mr. Buckingham pointed out, explaining why if the family moved to have Nat's will set aside and evict Maggie from the grand house Nat had paid every penny of himself, they would hurt Belinda and perhaps force her to choose between them and Maggie. And to their horror, eighteen-year-old Nat might choose Maggie, too.

"So, what do we do, father?" Nat's sister, Diana Buckingham Sterling, asked?

"Damned if I know, dear," her father replies. "I'm all conflicted. Besides, we don't know for sure if the insurance company will pay the ten million dollars considering it was Maggie's ex-husband and Belinda's father who murdered Nat."

"Well, I'm not confused," Diana's brother, Stephen, interjects. "Under the terms of Nat's will, Belinda will inherit millions and so will his son. She's well taken care of for the rest of her life, the way Nat wanted. I say we go after Maggie with everything our lawyers can throw at her. She can live in her damn car for all I care. I'm saying this case is still open because some new evidence could turn up. As a lawyer myself, I've seen it happen many times."

Observing the conversation is straying far beyond rational thought, Mr. Buckingham says: "Listen, everybody, perhaps this is not the time to deal with this matter. Under the circumstances, our grief may be doing the talking for us. We have plenty of time to take this up another day. I suggest each of us privately give some thought not to what we want but what we think Nat would have wanted us to do. I think we all would prefer to drop the whole matter and let Maggie live like the queen she wants to be rather than to drive a wedge between us and Belinda or Nat or both."

Chapter Thirty-One

Murder Affects Forrest and Olivia's Plans

"Is that the end of it, Forrest?" Olivia asks when he telephones to tell her the latest news about the murder charge against Maggie.

"I hope so, Olivia. If the district attorney is willing to accept LeRoy's confession and closes the case. He's a politically ambitious man, and he is being pushed by that detective, Chester Foy, whose hatred for Maggie's attorney might keep him investigating. Nat's family also still believes Maggie's guilty, and they have the money and the influence to keep pressuring the police and the DA's office."

"How's Belinda holding up? I talk to her on the phone every few days, and I know how much she is torn up and conflicted. She believes her mother is innocent, and yet she loved her stepfather dearly, and she even loved LeRoy despite all his flaws. The whole thing's just a damned shame."

"Yeah, it sure is. At any rate, it's going to take some time for Asher Heights to return to normal. And I'm sorry, Olivia, that you and I have been so personally affected. I was looking forward to the social events we had planned at the mansion, but I know you understand."

"I do, Forrest, and selfishly I have to admit I've missed the carefree times we had right after what I like to call our 'Greenbrier adventure'. When do you think we can get back to seeing each other regularly?"

"How's this weekend sound to you? I can fly to Chicago Friday and meet you for dinner as soon as you leave the office. Are you loaded with weekend work?"

"No, not too much. Let's just stay at my place so we can spend most of the time by ourselves. Think I can interest you in a weekend of kitchen and bedroom pleasures?" she teases.

"Depends on what's on the menu," Forrest jokes.

"You just might be surprised. Let's leave that to our imaginations. But before we hang up, the attorney part of me has a few questions about Maggie and her children."

"Let's hear them, Olivia. I'm not sure I have all the information, but fire away."

"First, what are Maggie's plans? Knowing human nature as I do, I suspect the town gossips and plenty of others still believe she paid Nat to get rid of a husband we all know she didn't love. Second, unless I'm mistaken, the insurance company will have to pay off the ten-million-dollar death benefit, and Maggie, Belinda, and Nat V will get their inheritance from Nat's will."

"I think you're right, Olivia. It appears Maggie will land on her feet once again. She'll finally have tons of money all to herself with no one to restrict how much she spends and what she spends it on. But for the children's sake, I'm glad they'll get their share. Nat did a really admirable job of taking care of them, and I'll always admire him for loving Belinda and treating her as if she were his biological daughter."

"But, Forrest, even with all that money can Maggie continue to live in Asher Heights? Will her friends stick with her? Will she still be welcome at the country club and be on the invitation list of the Asher Heights glitterati?"

"I really don't know. An ordinary person might admit defeat and leave town permanently, but Maggie is anything but ordinary. She just might have the audacity to stick it out.

"Anyway, see you this weekend?"

"Can't wait, my love."

* * *

Although Olivia's wisdom has guided her to be sympathetic and understanding, the interruptions caused by Nat's murder have interfered with their relationship. Even the timing itself is unfortunate, coming soon after the "Greenbrier adventure."

Forrest, however, has taken great pains to feed fuel to their passion. The lengths to which he goes are so uncharacteristic of his nature they both surprise and delight Olivia.

Every Monday two bunches of fresh flowers in collectable vases are delivered—one to her apartment and one to her office. The accompanying cards are not gushy, but "Love, Forrest" is a major milestone Olivia needs to hear.

Sending flowers is not what is uncharacteristic for Forrest. It's the other gifts that arrive unexpectedly at both her home and her place of work. Some are as playful as a wooden yo-yo with her initials carved on both sides; others, like birthstone earrings, reflect Forrest's generosity. All indicate he has taken the giant step into the romantic love that formerly frightened him.

None of the meaning of his efforts escapes Olivia.

Chapter Thirty-Two

Maggie's Freedom, Inheritance in Jeopardy

Stephen Buckingham was right when he insisted new evidence could turn up. Before Maggie has a chance to finish her plans for a get-away-from-it-all trip abroad, she is back in jail, charged again with the murder of her husband.

The arrest is based upon "new evidence" Prosecutor Adam Zeller said he believes will lead to her conviction. The source: LeRoy's brother Claude, currently serving a twenty-year armed robbery sentence in the maximum security prison at Mt. Olive. Zeller claims the brother has irrefutable proof Maggie Mullens Buckingham hired her former husband to kill Nat.

In an announcement to the news media, Zeller said: "We've confirmed Claude Bottoms was telling the truth when he led us to a box LeRoy buried in a shed behind his aunt Willa Dunkle's house. It contained the fifty thousand dollars Maggie Buckingham gave him as a down payment for killing her husband.

"When LeRoy found out he was dying sooner than he expected, he confessed the crime to Claude and told him where he hid the money. Claude is prepared to testify about when, where, and how the arrangement was made, and what the total payment was to be after Mrs. Buckingham collected Mr. Buckingham's life insurance money.

"We've asked the court for the earliest trial date possible."

***

Maggie is frantic. After LeRoy's confession that he was solely responsible for the murder, the insurance company was prepared to pay off the ten million dollar policy, and that, plus the millions Maggie would inherit from her late husband's estate, as well as several million more from the sale of the couple's house, would ensure her a rich lifestyle for as long as she lives.

Perplexed over how things could have gone so wrong, Maggie turns again for help from Gus McDermott, who, as always, is cockily confident he can make her troubles go away.

"The word of a convict, Maggie. That's all they have," Gus scoffs. "Hell's fire, Zeller's political ambitions must be scrambling his brains. You can bet the DA's offering Claude a huge deal to drastically reduce his sentence and maybe get him shifted to a minimum security prison. That'll be easy enough to find out. I'll make mincemeat out of that dunderhead when he takes the witness stand."

"That's what I thought, Gus," Maggie says. "But I'm worried Zeller's got something else going for him. Surely he's not foolish enough to base his case just on the word of someone like Claude. What else do you know?"

"Well, nothing at this point, Maggie. But I'm just getting started on the discovery phase, and I've turned my team of investigators loose. I'll know more in a few days. Right now, I'll focus on getting you out on bail."

"Yes, Gus. I don't care what the bail is; just get me out of here. You hear me?"

***

Maggie is right in suspecting Zeller has more to back up his case than Claude's word and the money found in the shed. He has subpoenas prepared for Maggie's closest friends with whom he has already confirmed she has discussed her unhappy marriage and how much she wanted to be free of Nat.

Zeller also knows from the husband of one of Maggie's friends that Maggie had a tubal ligation she never told Nat about. Zeller also plans to call to the stand her children, both of whom have witnessed years of arguments and tension between Maggie and Nat, as well as their use of separate bedrooms. They also are aware of how much time their elders deliberately spent apart from each other.

Members of Nat's family, especially his brother, are eager to testify they've always suspected Maggie seduced Nat into marrying her. "She never gave a damn about my brother," Stephen fumed in his interview with Zeller. "All she ever wanted was the Buckingham name and our money. Hell, it never took an Einstein to figure that out, Mr. Zeller. I loved my brother dearly, but it was quite evident he wasn't good-looking enough, charming enough, or popular enough to attract a beautiful young woman like Maggie. She teased him with sex to the point he'd give her anything to marry him. And that's precisely what she made him do. And then after she got everything he could give her, she plotted to get rid of him. Sir, I cannot wait to get on the witness stand!"

Zeller is counting on the cumulative effect of all the evidence, as circumstantial as it is, to convince a jury this woman of dubious reputation and a taste for high living couldn't wait for her husband's natural death to have it all to herself. He is so confident he can already see the letters on his new office door: Governor Adam Zeller.

That vision, however, is not shared by Gus McDermott, who is counting on Zeller to delude himself and thereby make himself vulnerable. "Zeller's got his convict witness; I'll just have to get one of my own, somebody who will testify that Claude bragged to him about getting a reduced sentence for involving Maggie in his brother's crime. Shouldn't be hard. Prisons are full of liars who'd sell their soul if you put enough money in front of them."

Gus figures his biggest problem is discovering where the money in the shed came from. "Sure as hell didn't come from LeRoy," Gus tells his longtime investigator, Logan Fernsby. "LeRoy and his brother Claude were both petty thieves and drug peddlers, Logan. Put together, they didn't have brains enough to accumulate five thousand dollars at one time, much less fifty thousand. And I believe LeRoy's confession that he killed Nat by himself. LeRoy wasn't completely stupid. He knew he could con his daughter out of plenty of money for the rest of his life. No, that money came from someone other than Maggie."

"Have any idea where to start looking, Gus?" Logan asks.

"Yeah, I do. But the list is going to be long to start with. Let's begin with the people who not only had the fifty grand to spare but also would be willing to spend it to see Maggie sent to jail for the rest of her life. That would include Nat's family, especially that brother who has been so outspoken in the press. What's his name?"

"Stephen, Gus. His name is Stephen. And you're right. He makes no secret of his hatred for her."

"OK, add to that list any women of Maggie's acquaintance who might be jealous of her beauty and the magnetic pull she has on the men in their snooty circle. Oh, and let's not overlook that super rich Alderson guy Maggie threw over years ago. Funny how he returned to Asher Heights not long before the murder after being gone all those years. It would be only human for him to want revenge. And seeing her sweet little avaricious ass dumped out of her big estate and into a six-by-eight prison cell would be most satisfying, I'm sure.

"And along the way," Gus smirks, "I don't mind at all making a small fortune out of this case and at the same time publicly kicking the shit out of Zeller and that asshole Detective Chester Foy."

Chapter Thirty-Three

"Scandalous" Public Trial Begins

On the first day of Maggie's trial, Asher Heights all but ceases functioning as a city. Everyone from the most prominent citizens to those of modest circumstances competes for seats in the courtroom. Local news media reporters are joined by others from throughout West Virginia, and even a few from national newspapers and broadcast companies.

This case has the sensational elements for wide audience appeal: scandal, powerful families, a social climbing money-hungry alleged husband killer, millions in life insurance and inheritance, a politically ambitious prosecutor, and a flamboyant defense attorney with a reputation for spellbinding juries into letting the guilty escape unpunished.

In his opening statement to the jury, Adam Zeller, who is risking his future trying this career-making case himself, enumerates every reason why Maggie Mullens Buckingham is guilty of the first-degree murder of her husband and why the jury must do its sworn duty and convict her.

She never loved Broderick Nathanial Buckingham IV, Zeller insists. She made him irrational, taunting him with the promise of a lifetime of sexual pleasure from the kind of beautiful, sensual woman who had spurned him since his early teen years. Nat's family saw her from the beginning as an opportunist interested only in wealth and social status, a woman who cared nothing for Nat but used him to achieve her own selfish goals. Her best friends, those in whom she confided, knew she was sickened by having to endure martial relations with him but was tied to him by a prenuptial agreement that left her only a hundred thousand dollars if she divorced him—a large sum of money to most people but a pittance to Maggie who records will show could burn through that much money in no time at all.

And then the clincher. Claude Bottoms's testimony that his brother LeRoy confessed to him Maggie gave him a fifty-thousand-dollar down payment to kill Nat. "To back that up," Zeller emphasizes with appropriate pausing and dramatic flair, "that money was retrieved by officials from my office, and I'm going to bring it into this courtroom and show it to you."

With that final hammering of his statement, Zeller looks individually into the eyes of each juror, gives them a nod of his head, and takes his seat.

Gus rises energetically from his chair at the defense table, buttons his dark blue custom-tailored suit complemented by a red, white, and blue striped tie and a matching pocket square, and struts from one end of the jury box to the other, smiling and nodding confidently at each juror, leaving the impression his remarks are intended solely for that individual.

"Ladies and gentlemen," Gus begins, "the honorable prosecutor has presented an impressive case against my client, Maggie Buckingham. He paints her as a black widow who devours her mate after she has gotten all the use out of him she wants. He purports to back up those claims by threatening to call her friends and family members and force them to testify against her. And then he plans to bring in the confessed killer's brother, a convict named Claude Bottoms, as his crowning glory to put the finishing touches on his prosecution.

"I admit, ladies and gentleman . . . I freely admit I wouldn't blame you if each of you is pretty well convinced she's guilty. Except for one insurmountable problem Mr. Zeller has. And that problem is this: None of what he claims is true.

"Any complaints about her husband Maggie made in confidence to her friends are the same complaints every other woman who has ever been a wife has made at one time or another over the years about her husband. But we all know most often spouses are just temporarily upset and need to vent.

"As far as Maggie's entrapping Nat Buckingham for her own selfish ends, let me point out that Mr. Buckingham was an unusually intelligent man with a degree from an Ivy League university and a well-deserved reputation as a skillful businessman who earned millions of dollars for himself, his family, and his investors. Now, does that sound like a man who would be so utterly naïve and gullible he could be easily fooled by anyone, man or woman? I don't think so.

"Considering the prosecutor's claim that Maggie married Nat only for his fortune and prominent family name, let me ask you this: Why did she stay married to him for nineteen years if she was so miserably unhappy? They had a child, Broderick Nathaniel Buckingham V, near the end of their first year of marriage. Maggie could have divorced Nat then, received the prenuptial settlement of one hundred thousand dollars, plus many thousands of dollars a month in child support for the next seventeen years until her son reached the age of a legal adult, at which time he stood to inherit millions of his own. Her luxurious lifestyle would hardly have changed at all.

"Also take into account the fact that the most important part of Mr. Zeller's case, as well as the only reason he was able to recharge my client, is the statement of a lifelong felon, a petty thief who peddled drugs on street corners and in alleys. I submit that Claude Bottoms, like his late brother LeRoy, wasn't even smart enough to steal enough money or sell enough drugs to support himself without living on food stamps and government handouts.

"Finally, Maggie Buckingham should never have been charged again because she was completely exonerated by her first husband, LeRoy Bottoms, who made a deathbed confession that he was solely responsible for the murder of Nat Buckingham, and he specifically stated Maggie had nothing to do with it. She did not hire him. She did not pay him. She disliked him so much she had nothing to do with him after their divorce. The fact is, she knew absolutely nothing about any plan to kill Nat Buckingham until she discovered her husband's dead body.

"You are doubtlessly asking yourself if you can take the word of a career criminal like LeRoy Bottoms when I've already pointed out that you should not take the word of his brother, Claude, also a lifelong felon. Yes, you can, and here's why. LeRoy and Maggie's daughter, Belinda, is known by all of her family, her friends, her co-workers, her acquaintances, and especially her clergy as an extremely devout Christian who committed herself during her father's last months of life to saving his immortal soul. And she was successful. LeRoy died a forgiven Christian. Why then would he renounce his conversion and acceptance of Jesus Christ as his personal savior by lying and implicating his daughter's mother one week before he died?

"That one consideration alone is enough for you to justify your finding my client, Maggie Buckingham, not guilty and returning her to the life she deserves with her daughter, her son, and the rest of her family and friends."

* * *

Knowing Olivia will be eager to hear what direction the prosecutor and the defense attorney appear to be taking the trial, Forrest has clippings from the Asher Heights newspaper faxed to her daily, and he calls every evening.

"Not a whole lot to report about the first day, Olivia, except this little town hasn't seen anything quite like this before. The trial's all anybody is talking about.

"Maggie's attorney, Gus McDermott, seems confident. He has a big reputation in these parts, and he's a real showman in the courtroom. Expensive suit, flashy tie, big smile, cocky strut in front of the jurors. Put on quite a performance today.

"The prosecutor might as well be wearing an 'I'm-running-for-governor sandwich board sign'. It's so obvious why he is arguing the case instead of assigning it to his assistants, as he does with ordinary cases. He's going to go all out, and that means he's going to use all the dirt on Maggie he can uncover or imply.

"It's going to be nasty; that's for sure. I feel sorry for Belinda and young Nat. Hell of a thing for them to have to go through. Same for the Buckingham family. Maggie, on the other hand, looks strong, proud, and defiant. She may be scared inside, but that's not what the jury is seeing."

"Forrest, do you think Belinda is in the right frame of mind for me to call her tonight? I'd feel better if I could speak with her."

"She'd appreciate hearing from you, I'm sure."

"OK, I'll call her right now. Thanks for the update, Forrest. Talk to you tomorrow night?"

"Absolutely."

Chapter Thirty-Four

Witnesses Damage Maggie

Prosecutor Zeller's first witness is Dr. Letishia Freeman, the forensic pathologist who examined Nat's body at the scene of the crime and also conducted the autopsy. Her testimony is routine, establishing what is already known and not challenged by either Zeller or McDermott. Dr. Freeman confirms death was caused by a single stab wound to the heart sometime between one and three a.m.

His next witness is definitely prejudiced toward the prosecution. Detective Chester Foy is convinced Maggie is guilty, despises her attorney, and Zeller's questions are intended to create as much damage to the defense as possible.

"Detective Foy, would you please describe the defendant's physical appearance when you arrived at the Buckingham house on the morning of the murder."

"Mrs. Buckingham was dressed in a houserobe, long nightgown, and slippers. The robe was open, and I observed blood stains on the front of her nightgown, and on her hands."

"Did you ask her how the blood happened to get on her clothing?"

"Yes sir. She said she didn't know. She said she could not remember anything between the time she went to bed and when she discovered Mr. Buckingham's dead body about six-thirty."

"On what basis did you arrest her and charge her with her husband's murder?"

"She was covered in her husband's blood. She had no explanation about how it got there. There was no evidence at all of a forced entry, and the knife was from her own kitchen. Besides, it's common knowledge they had a rocky marriage."

"Objection, your honor," McDermott shouts.

"Sustained" Judge Jackson McKnight rules. "The jury will disregard Mr. Foy's last remark. Do you have any further questions for this witness, Mr. Zeller?"

"No, your honor."

McDermott certainly does. He springs to his feet and walks with considerable energy, looking at each juror on his way to face Foy.

"Mr. Foy, you said Mrs. Buckingham had blood on her clothing, but you mentioned nothing about her robe. Did it also have blood on it?"

"No, it did not. But I asked her to remove it, and she did. That's when I saw blood all over the front of her gown and on the sleeves. She evidently put on the robe after she found her husband's body and before the police arrived."

Foy has answered just as McDermott had wanted. He designed his follow-up questions to provide a logical, innocent reason for the blood stains.

"Detective, did you observe any blood on the back of her gown?"

"No," he has to admit.

"Your report states, and the medical examiner agrees, there was no sign of a struggle, that Mr. Buckingham was not awake when he was stabbed. I ask you, therefore, could the blood possibly have gotten on Mrs. Buckingham's clothing because she clung to him in her grief after determining he was indeed dead?"

Foy says nothing, just stares at McDermott making no effort to hide his intense dislike for him.

"One last question, Mr. Foy. Were Mrs. Buckingham's fingerprints on the murder weapon? Without waiting for a reply, McDermott says,

"The answer is no, and I have no further questions for this witness, your honor." He nods triumphantly at the jurors and takes his seat.

Zeller then begins his attempt to use Maggie's friends and family to establish that she had a sham of a marriage and desperately wanted to end it without losing all the millions of dollars through her connection to the Buckingham family. He calls Priscilla Claymoore Amsbury, a member of Maggie's circle of close friends.

"Mrs. Amsbury, would you please explain the nature of your relationship with the defendant, Maggie Mullens Buckingham."

"Mrs. Buckingham is a friend."

"A close friend, one with whom you frequently socialize, Mrs. Amsbury?"

"Yes, and we have a number of friends in common."

"Have you and Mrs. Buckingham ever had personal conversations, discussing matters intended to remain between the two of you?"

"Objection, your honor," McDermott interrupts. "Relevance?"

"Objection overruled, Mr. McDermott," the judge replies in a calm and even voice. "The question seems appropriate. You may answer, Mrs. Amsbury."

"I'm not sure specifically what I am being asked, but, yes, we have had private conversations."

"Has Mrs. Buckingham ever expressed to you any dissatisfaction she had in her marriage to Mr. Buckingham?"

"Same objection," McDermitt says again.

"Overruled, but, Mr. Zeller, get to the point of your questioning. Please answer, Mrs. Amsbury."

"Yes," she responds tersely.

"Did Mrs. Buckingham ever say to you that she would like to get out of her marriage? Please answer yes or no."

"Yes, but it usually followed a fuss between her and her husband, and I did not know if she really meant it."

"Please, Mrs. Amsbury," the judge interrupts, "just stick to the facts as you know them and refrain from adding your opinions."

"Yes, your honor."

"One final question, Mrs. Amsbury. As a good friend of the defendant's, and as one in whom she confided, did Mrs. Buckingham ever discuss with you the subject of her martial relations with her husband?"

"Objection, your honor," McDermott shouts.

"I'll allow a little leeway," Judge McKnight answers, "but, Mr. Zeller, you know the limitations of such questioning. Do not cross over the line."

"Yes, sir. Thank you, your honor. Now, Mrs. Amsbury, please, your answer?"

"Maggie, that is, Mrs. Buckingham, did tell me that that part of her relationship with Mr. Buckingham had deteriorated over time."

"Did Mrs. Buckingham ever talk about having more children?"

"Yes, she said one son and one daughter completed her family as far as she was concerned. Besides, she couldn't have more children anyway."

No sooner had the words escaped her mouth than Mrs. Amsbury regretted saying them. She instantly realized how damaging her admission could be because she knew Maggie had not told Nat.

Zeller, on the other hand, had to strain mightily to keep from shouting "Hallelujah!" He knew about the operation but did not think the judge would let him get away with asking about it. The revelation was a gift from the gods that prosecutors always wish for but rarely receive. He hurries his next question even though he knows the judge will strike it down and admonish him for asking it.

"Did Mrs. Buckingham admit to you she immediately had a son to make sure she'd always have a strong tie to the Buckingham fortune, and then deceived her husband into believing she could have more children?" Zeller immediately got the warning he knew was coming. But the mild dressing down he received from the judge was well worth it.

"Do you have questions, Mr. McDermott?"

"I do, your honor."

Looking slowly into the faces of the jurors as he approaches the witness, McDermott, says, "I have only a few questions, Mrs. Amsbury. So please bear with me."

"Tell me, is Mrs. Buckingham your only friend who has ever complained to you about her marriage?"

"No. All of my close friends have vented about their spouses from time to time."

"Does that include you, Mrs. Amsbury?" McDermott chuckles while looking not at the witness but at the jurors."

"I'm afraid so."

"But you, like Mrs. Buckingham, remained married?"

"Yes, I have indeed."

"Did Mrs. Buckingham ever say to you she married her husband for his money and for his family's prestigious name?"

"No, she did not."

"Mrs. Amsbury, the prosecutor implied to the jury that Mrs. Buckingham did not want her son but had him only for the child support money she would get if her husband divorced her. Did she ever say anything to you to indicate there's any truth in that claim?"

"Absolutely not. She dearly loves her son."

"Has Mrs. Buckingham ever said to you that she wanted to have her husband murdered?"

"No, never."

"One last question, Mrs. Amsbury. You have testified that all your close friends, and even you yourself have vented to one another when you were angry with your husbands. So, tell me, have you or anyone else in your circle of friends ever plotted to have their husbands murdered?"

The question annoys both the prosecutor and the judge, who pounds his gavel to bring order from the spectators, who, as McDermott anticipated, were amused by the question.

"I withdraw the question, your honor," McDermott hastily adds. "I have no more questions for this witness."

"You will not have questions for any witness if you pull another stunt like that in my courtroom, Mr. McDermott. Do not test me again, sir." Turning to the jurors, Judge McKnight orders them to disregard that last question, but, as McDermott, Zeller, and everyone else knows, there is no way jurors can forget the question and its implications.

Zeller decides against questioning the four other friends of Maggie's he has subpoenaed. They can only reinforce Mrs. Ambury's testimony confirming Maggie was unhappy in her marriage. He does not want to risk their being tricked by "that unscrupulous bastard Gus McDermott" into saying or implying something damaging.

The first day ends with each side striking a blow to impress the jury. McDermott made clear that Maggie's prints were not on the knife and raised reasonable doubt about how blood got on her clothing. In addition, his questioning of Mrs. Amsbury left the impression, he hoped, that Maggie's complaints about her marriage were no different from those of her friends, and that she had never said anything to indicate she'd like to see Nat dead, much less had plotted his death.

Mrs. Amsbury's slip about Maggie's operation made Zeller's day. He left court feeling even more confident about a conviction he could use as a stepping stone to the governor's mansion.

154

Chapter Thirty-Five

Prosecutor Subpoenas Maggie's Children

At the beginning of Maggie's trial, her children faced a dilemma that defied a unified solution: Where to sit in the courtroom?

Should both Belinda and Nat sit near the defense table, which would signal their support for their mother? Or with the Buckingham family on the other side of the courtroom, indicating their support for the prosecution? They were caught between the proverbial rock and a hard place.

With Forrest's counsel, they choose a compromise. Belinda meets with the Buckinghams, reassures them of her genuine love, but asks them to understand she must sit on her mother's side. Not because she has any less love for her late stepfather, but because she believes her mother had nothing to do with the murder. Nat will alternate, sitting one day with the Buckinghams and the next with Belinda. Forrest, who had no intention of witnessing the trial in person, nevertheless would not think of having Belinda sitting without moral support every other day of the trial. He will be with her when Nat is not.

The Buckinghams accept the compromise with mixed feelings. The grandparents are understanding; Uncle Stephen is not. He resents Maggie so much he cannot understand why Nat would even consider sitting on her side for one moment, much less every other day. Aunt Diana advises Belinda and Nat to do what they think is right for them. That's what she plans to do. And "right" for her is not attending until the day of the verdict. She cannot tolerate the stress.

What no one anticipates is the considerable controversy Forrest's presence beside Belinda creates. The town's older tongue-waggers who remember the scandalous breakup between Maggie and Forrest recirculate the story for anyone who will listen. Worse, they add their own vicious speculation. Is Forrest still in love with Maggie? Did Forrest give Maggie the money to hire LeRoy to kill her husband so he could have her back? Did Maggie plot the murder on her own in hopes of winning Forrest back after he returned home an extremely wealthy man living in a fabulous mansion? Is Forrest romantically involved with Belinda? Could it be that Forrest is Belinda's real father?

When Forrest recounts all of this to Olivia on the telephone, she is incensed.

"How insensitive and unfair to you and Belinda and even Nat. Aren't those kids suffering enough already. I'm sorry for all of you, Forrest, for having to put up with such hurtful nonsense. But I'm damn proud of you for shielding them as much as you've been able to. I'm very much aware you could have stayed very comfortably at home and ignored the whole business."

What Forrest doesn't burden Olivia with is the attention he draws by just appearing in public. Everybody has driven past the grand mansion and is amazed at how magnificent it looks. Everybody is fascinated by him and wondering what his plans are. He has unwittingly become a celebrity.

As for Maggie, she doesn't give a hoot about the Buckinghams and wants to have both children on her side the entire time. But she loves them too much to complain and add to their discomfort. Fortunately, she does get to see and talk with them all they want because Gus managed to post a high enough bail to gain home confinement for her. Both Belinda and Nat visit regularly.

Now Belinda and Nat's carefully crafted compromise about where to sit is being rocked by Adam Zeller. He has subpoenaed both as witnesses for the prosecution.

***

Zeller wants to build as strong a case against Maggie as he possibly can before he calls his key witness, Claude Bottoms, whose character and reputation will undoubtedly make his testimony suspect with the jury.

Zeller is counting on Belinda Bottoms to be one hundred percent truthful even though she is a most reluctant witness. He knows her desire to protect her mother cannot overcome her faithfulness as a Christian. Zeller has prepared questions designed to make Belinda's responses seem worse than they actually are.

"Ms. Bottoms, please state the nature of your relationship with the defendant, Maggie Bottoms Buckingham."

"She is my mother."

"And your relationship to the deceased, Broderick Nathaniel Buckingham IV?"

"My stepfather."

"How would you describe your relationship with your mother? How do you get along?"

"We get along as well as most daughters and mothers, I suppose. I know we love each other, and she has always been generous with me and provided for me."

"Do you spend much time together? Attending church? Going shopping? Visiting each other? Talking on the telephone? In other words, are you close?"

"We talk regularly, and I occasionally have a meal at her house, or meet her at a restaurant."

"Do you confide in each other? Trust each other with your most private information?"

"No. I can't say that we do that."

"What about your stepfather? How was your relationship with him?"

"I loved him very much. He always made time for me and treated me as if I were his biological daughter."

"How old were you when your mother and stepfather were married?"

"I was four."

"So, you lived with your mother and your stepfather for almost twenty years before you graduated from college and moved into a separate residence."

"That is correct."

"From your observations during all that time, how would you characterize the relationship between Mr. and Mrs. Buckingham? Did they, in your opinion, have a close, loving marriage?"

"Sometimes."

"More often than not, would you say?"

"No sir."

"Did you observe them quarreling regularly?

"Yes."

"Can you provide some examples of what they argued about?"

"Nat complained about how much money my mother spent, about how much time she spent away from home, and that we did not do enough together as a family. Mother complained about Nat's spending so much time at the office, often working weekends and holidays, and not taking her to as many social events as she wanted to attend."

"Did they share the same bedroom, Ms. Bottoms? Please answer yes or no.

"I can't answer yes or no. Neither is totally accurate. My truthful answer is I do not remember if they did when I was a child, but since I've been an adult, I'd say each has a bedroom, but they sometimes share one."

"Did you ever hear them discuss whether they wanted to have more children than you and your brother?"

"Once or twice that I recall. Nat said he'd like to have more, and mother told him it was up to 'Mother Nature,' who didn't seem to be cooperating."

* * *

When Zeller called Maggie and Nat's son to the stand, Zeller questioned him along the same lines as he had Belinda. Nat explained he loved his parents and was treated well by them. When asked about his relationship with Belinda, his *half-sister,* he bristled at the characterization.

"Belinda and I don't make such distinctions, sir. I couldn't ask for a better sister, and I couldn't possibly love her any more than I do."

Anticipating this response, Zeller asked what he expected to be a damaging question. "When you are troubled or need advice, whom do you turn to most, your mother or your sister?"

Nat looked stricken. He was intelligent and quick-minded enough to recognize he has been steered by Zeller to an answer that could cause the jury to look even more negatively toward his mother. Nat gave a clever answer, one that would avoid the trap he had been led into.

"I depend on advice from my mother for things an older person would know about and Belinda for things a younger person would understand better."

However, Nat could not dodge Zeller's questions centering on the relationship between his mother and father, their quarreling, and their separate bedrooms. When asked if he had ever told his mother and father he would like to have a brother or another sister, he said yes, but he had never heard his mother and father discuss this subject.

Both Belinda and Nat left the courtroom depressed because they could not tell the jury their parents were deeply in love and got along wonderfully. They both had the impression the jurors had very little sympathy for their mother and that Gus McDermott's cross-examination of them did not have much influence.

Chapter Thirty-Six

Claude Has His Day in Court

Over the strenuous objections of Gus McDermott, Adam Zeller was able to persuade Judge McKnight to permit Claude Bottoms to exchange his prison uniform for a suit and tie, thus potentially reducing the prejudice individual jurors might have if they were constantly reminded by prison garb that Claude is a convict—something the defense had been hoping to use to its advantage.

So, when Claude was sworn in, he looked downright dapper, freshly shaved with a neatly trimmed mustache, and wearing a dark blue suit, red and blue silk tie, and shiny black shoes. Instead of a felon, he had the appearance of a man who had just attended a church service. The jury was not seeing the real Claude, precisely what Zeller had intended and exactly what McDermott and the defense did not want.

Zeller's tactics were to skim over the damaging testimony as quickly as possible, giving the jurors as little time as he could to dwell on it.

"Mr. Bottoms," Zeller began, "you currently are an inmate at the Mount Olive Correctional Complex, are you not?" Zeller carefully avoided more negative words like prisoner, criminal, penitentiary and prison.

"Yes."

"What is the nature of your offense?"

"Robbery."

Zeller let the matter drop with those one-word responses, and both avoided saying "armed" before "robbery," just as they had rehearsed.

"Tell the court, please, Mr. Bottoms, your relationship with the late LeRoy Bottoms.

"He was my brother."

"And the defendant is your former sister-in-law?"

"That is correct, sir."

"And how long have you known Mrs. Buckingham?"

"Well, let's see. I reckon it's been almost twenty-five years. I met her a little while before they was married. But I haven't seen or talked tuh her in more than twenty years, as far as I can recollect."

"Did you know her second husband, Broderick Nathaniel Buckingham IV?"

"No, sir."

"You never met him or communicated with him in any way?"

"No, sir."

"When did you first become aware your brother LeRoy claimed he was hired to murder Mr. Buckingham?"

"Just before he became too weak to travel. He come tuh see me at Mt. Olive. There was somethin' urgent he wanted tuh tell me before he died."

"And that was what, Mr. Bottoms?"

"That he killed Mr. Buckingham and had fifty thousand dollars buried in our Aunt Willa Dunkle's shed behind her house."

McDermott sits quietly. Objecting would be futile because police have already found the money.

"And did your brother say how he got this money and who it came from?"

"From Maggie. She give him the money as a down payment fer murderin' her husband. LeRoy said she promised tuh pay him a million more onced she got the life insurance money."

Now McDermott objects. Loudly. He bounds out of his chair, takes a couple of steps toward the judge, and yells: "Objection. Heresay, your honor. There's no way he can prove Mrs. Buckingham did any such thing."

"You'll get your chance to refute the statement on cross, Mr. McDermott. As for you, Mr. Zeller, I've warned you before. As an experienced prosecutor, you know better."

To the jury, Judge McKnight says, "You may consider the testimony about the fifty thousand dollars and where it was found, but unless proof to the contrary is offered, the testimony about what Mrs. Buckingham did or did not say, or did or did not do is disallowed."

However, Zeller had made his point, and everyone from the judge to the defense attorney to the jurors damn well knew it. The damage had been done—just as Zeller had set it up.

"One last question, Mr. Bottoms. Why did you alert my office about the fifty thousand dollars? Weren't you tempted to leave the money where it was until you could get it for yourself when your sentence was up?"

"That was temptin', and if I was gittin' out anytime soon, I mighta done just that. But I got eleven years left tuh serve, and I'd like tuh git out sooner than that."

"So, you figured you could make some kind of deal with my office to get your sentence reduced?"

"Yes, sir."

"Well, how did that work out for you."

"You said you'd consider it."

"But I made no promises, correct."

"Correct."

***

Because the time is approaching five p.m., Judge McKnight adjourns until nine a.m. the next day, which would seem to be a disadvantage to Gus McDermott and the defense because Claude Bottoms had just given testimony that needed to be refuted and discredited before the jury had all night to let what he testified to sink in. However, McDermott had already planned to take the somewhat unusual step of delaying his cross-examination. Claude was the prosecution's last witness, and Gus had some groundwork to lay before confronting Claude.

When court resumed the following morning, McDermott called in a vice president of the First National Bank, in which Nat and Maggie had accounts. Henry P. Waldorph explained that Mr. Buckingham had checking and savings accounts in his name only, and that Mrs. Buckingham had only a checking account that also was registered in Mr. Buckingham's name, giving both of them access not only to the money but also the records of when deposits and withdrawals were made, as well as a copy of all checks written. The account, he testified, never had more than twenty-five thousand dollars in it at any time.

Next, he called Nat's personal attorney who oversaw an accounting firm that handled all of Nat's financial affairs. Jeffrey Ironton explained that Nat tightly controlled Mrs. Buckingham's access to money. He provided one thousand dollars a month in cash in addition to her access to the joint checking account. Nat's purpose was not only to control the amount of money Mrs. Buckingham spent, but also to keep her from accumulating a large enough sum of money to tempt her to divorce him and also collect the one hundred thousand dollars as stipulated under the prenuptial agreement.

"Considering your testimony, Mr. Ironton, do you think Mrs. Buckingham could accumulate fifty thousand dollars in cash and keep it hidden from Mr. Buckingham?" Zeller objected, citing speculation, but Judge McKnight allowed Ironton to answer.

"No," he said. "My records over the nineteen years of their marriage indicate Mrs. Buckingham spent everything she could every month."

Zeller countered with one question only. "Isn't it possible, Mr. Ironton, that in a family as enormously wealthy as the Buckinghams, that Maggie Buckingham could hide an average of only two hundred twenty dollars a month for nineteen years, and thereby accumulate fifty thousand dollars in cash?"

"Yes. I suppose that is possible," Ironton responded.

Now, McDermott was ready to attack Claude Bottoms's testimony and hope he could find some open minds on the jury after Claude's rather convincing performance the day before.

"Mr. Bottoms, you testified yesterday that you are serving a twenty-year prison term for robbery, did you not?"

"Yes, sir."

"Didn't you and the prosecutor conveniently omit that it was not a simple robbery but *armed* robbery? Robbery under the threat of a handgun brandished in the face of your victim?"

"Answer the question," Judge McKnight orders after Claude sits silent.

"Yes, sir. That is correct."

"You also said yesterday that you voluntarily contacted the police and told them about the fifty thousand dollars buried in your aunt's shed, as opposed to keeping it for yourself upon your release from prison?"

"Yes, sir."

"Did you volunteer this information out of the kindness of your heart or a sense of civic responsibility? Or did you exchange it for something in return from the prosecutor's office?"

Claude says nothing again.

"Don't bother," McDermott instructs. "I believe the question answers itself. Now, Mr. Bottoms, please tell the jury what you are receiving in return."

"As I testified yesterday, Mr. Zeller made no promises."

"But you're here testifying today, so tell us what he said he might be able to do without promising."

As Zeller rose to object, Judge McKnight said, "Don't bother. The witness will answer the question."

"Mr. Zeller said he would personally appear on my behalf at my parole hearing later this year and explain that I helped solve a murder case and bring justice to the victim's family."

"Is that all, Mr. Bottoms? Remember you are under oath. You do not want to commit perjury and add more years to the sentence you are now serving."

"He said he'd do his best to get me transferred to a minimum security prison and made a trustee with more privileges."

"So, your accusation against my client carried a price tag for the prosecutor?"

"Objection!" Zeller signals.

Before Judge McKnight could draw breath to make a ruling, McDermott presented another of his bottomless supply of "I-withdraw-the-question" responses.

"Mr. Bottoms, I see from your police record you've been arrested more than a dozen times since you were eighteen years old and have been convicted of several misdemeanors and two felonies. You've spent time in several county and regional jails and two prison sentences. Is that accurate?"

"I guess."

"So, it's fair to surmise you've been involved in criminal activity all your adult life?"

When Claude sits silent again, McDermott continues. "No need to answer that question. I'm through with this witness, your honor."

"Mr. McDermott, we have only about forty-five minutes before the lunch recess. Do you anticipate needing more time than that with your next witness?"

"No, sir. I call Mrs. Willa Dunkle to the stand?"

Looking dignified in an inexpensive but neat and freshly pressed dress she usually wears to church, Mrs. Dunkle is sworn in and sits. She has been "prepped" by McDermott's assistants and is prepared "to do my duty."

"Good morning, Mrs. Dunkle," McDermott begins in a friendly manner. "Thank you for appearing today. I have just a few questions regarding your nephews, LeRoy and Claude Bottoms. I understand they are the sons of your late sister, Esther Bottoms?"

"That's correct. And I know them well. I helped my sister raise them after her husband died and she had to go to work to support them. And I'm sorry to say neither one turned out the way their mother and I wanted them to."

"You took care of LeRoy in your home the last months of his life, did you not?"

"Yes, I did.

"Did LeRoy tell you about murdering Mr. Buckingham?"

"Not until he told his daughter, Belinda, he wanted to confess the murder to the police as the last thing he did to get right with God. LeRoy died less than a week later."

"Did you hear him swear that the defendant, his former wife Maggie Buckingham, was not involved and did not hire him to kill her husband?"

"Yes, sir. No doubt about that. He made that point clear. I'm grateful and proud to say he died at peace with God."

"Then how do you account for Claude's tale about LeRoy visiting him at the prison, telling him Maggie hired him to kill Mr. Buckingham, and hiding the money in your shed."

"I love Claude, Mr. McDermott, just as I loved LeRoy. But Claude's lying. I don't blame him the least little bit for wanting to get out of prison sooner, but if LeRoy had money like that, he would have found a way of taking some of it and helping out our situation. We were downright poor while he was dying because of the medical expenses. We were using house payment and grocery money to pay for his pain pills and other prescriptions. I had to get help from my church to keep us fed.

"LeRoy—and Claude, too, for that matter—knew I'd never accept any ill-gotten money, so I'm certain LeRoy would never tell me if he had fifty thousand dollars. But he could have made up some excuse I would have believed about coming into a few hundred. LeRoy had many faults that I knew all too well, but he loved me, and I know he never would have left me with the pile of debts I have because of his cancer. No, sir. He'd never had done that to me. He was too grateful for that."

"Did you see LeRoy bury the money in your shed or notice any place in the building where the ground had recently been disturbed?"

"No, sir. First of all, LeRoy didn't have the strength, and I hardly ever go into that shed. Somebody buried that money there, but it wasn't LeRoy because he was too weak to do any digging."

"Thank you, Mrs. Dunkle."

Zeller had two questions in his cross-examination, and they forced Mrs. Dunkle to admit she could not testify with absolute certainly that Claude was lying or that LeRoy didn't bury the money before his illness incapacitated him. Zeller hoped that would help undo the harm her testimony had done his case. He had not objected at the beginning of her testimony when she said Claude was lying because he did not want the jurors to think he was attacking a witness they obviously admired.

* * *

In his nightly telephone conversation with Olivia, Forrest has one report for her that gives him optimism and another that disgusts him.

"Start with the optimistic one, Forrest. I think I'd like to hear that first."

"All right, it's this. As you know, Olivia, I have no legal training, but it seems to me that Zeller's case depends on the jury believing Claude's story, helped along by the district attorney doing everything he can to smear Maggie—without regard to whether any of it is true. If it weren't for the fact that Claude is a convict, I think the jury would believe him. Maybe they'll believe him anyway.

"McDermott, on the other hand, had a very credible witness in Claude and LeRoy's aunt. She came across as a very righteous elderly lady who quietly refuted everything Claude said while simultaneously expressing her love for him. I think she made a real impact on the jurors. That's the good news."

"OK, Forrest. What's disgusting you?"

"The damn attorneys, including the judge. I know you're not a trial lawyer, Olivia, but you went to law school, same as they did. Help me understand a few things. I mean, I'm a fairly sophisticated middle-aged man with a good education. I've been around long enough not to be too naïve, but this is the first trial I've witnessed in person. And what I've seen does somewhat disgust me."

"Like what?" Olivia inquires.

"Like why defense attorneys put getting their client off above any consideration for their guilt or innocence. Like trying to put the blame on someone else they know for certain is innocent. Like phrasing questions in such a way that they elicit answers that distort the facts. Like saying things they know will be stricken from the record just so the jury can be misled by them.

"And by prosecutors dead set on convicting the defendant even though they may have serious doubts about his or her guilt. By trying to suppress testimony or records that might favor the defendant? By asking loaded questions that are intended to mislead the jury instead of getting at the truth.

"Isn't seeing that justice is done supposed to be the purpose of a trial?'

"That's the judge's role, Forrest. It is the defense attorney's job to get a not guilty verdict, and the prosecutor is supposed to get a conviction."

"Then why do judges allow attorneys to say things or ask questions that all of them know are improper? They have contempt power to stop that. And who's kidding whom about things stricken from the record? How can jurors disregard information just because the judge tells them to?

"No disrespect to you as an attorney, but I don't know how some defense attorneys and prosecutors live with themselves."

"I agree the system is not perfect, Forrest. I just hope for Maggie's and her children's sake, she gets a fair trial."

"Guess we'll see, Olivia."

Chapter Thirty-Seven

The Fifty Thousand Dollar Solution

McDermott and his chief investigator, Logan Fernsby, were frustrated in their attempts to track down the person who provided the fifty thousand dollars. That one element, more than any other, ties Maggie to the murder. Neither LeRoy nor Claude had anywhere near such a sum. Gus and Logan believe Maggie didn't have that much cash either, considering how her husband controlled the amount of money she had access to. So where did it come from?

They considered the new guy in town, Maggie's extraordinarily rich former boyfriend, Forrest Alderson. He undoubtedly had the cash, many times over. But even though Forrest could logically be thought to hate Maggie for dumping him, that was many years ago. Besides, Maggie had assured them she and Forrest had reconciled their differences, or at least had determined to be civil to each other. Plus, Forrest had become very fond of Maggie's daughter and would not want to harm her by framing her mother for murder and having her locked away for the remainder of her life.

That left several Buckingham family members as the potential source. After Nat's death and Maggie's first arrest, Nat's father, sister, and especially his brother, Stephen, spoke publicly of their dislike for Maggie and about their steadfast conviction she was guilty.

"Every adult member of that family has the money to frame Maggie," Logan knew, "and I've been trying to tie one or more of them to it. But there's just no trail, no records to show any of them had made a fifty-thousand-dollar withdrawal from a bank account, from selling stock or property, or anything."

"So, we're at a dead end, then?" McDermott asks dejectedly.

"Not altogether, Gus. Not if you are willing to run a bluff."

"How so?"

"I've found out that one of Claude's former cellmates is Christopher Slatterly, and Christopher Slatterly's lawyer is none other than Stephen Buckingham."

"Go on," Gus urges, allowing himself to get hopeful.

"Well, if Claude is lying, as we are convinced he is, someone other than LeRoy had to bribe or otherwise influence him to say what he did to the police. LeRoy insisted on his deathbed Maggie had no part in the murder.

"So, two weeks after LeRoy's death, prison records show Slatterly visited Claude. Since he's been out of prison, that's the one and only time he went to see Claude. So, we can figure the two are not exactly close. Then one day after that visit, LeRoy sells his story to the police and Zeller's office and they arrest Maggie again."

"Hot damn!" McDermott rejoices. "I smell reasonable doubt all the way from here to the U.S. Supreme Court, Logan. We can't prove Stephen provided the money and enlisted Slatterly to persuade Claude to go along with the scheme, but I'm betting everything it's believable to at least one member of any jury in the land. And we need only one vote to have a hung jury. But I'm even more optimistic than that. I think we can win an acquittal."

"But, Gus, do you really believe Stephen will cave in on the witness stand and admit what he did.?"

"Hell, no. He's way too smart for that. The key is not to tip him off. To catch him off guard. Not give him a chance to huddle up with a bunch of his lawyer friends and plot some clever denials. As you know, I already have Nat's father, mother, sister, and brother under subpoenas I issued at the beginning of the trial. I had no plans to call them, but I wanted them on my witness list, just in case. By now, at this point in the trial, they must be feeling confident they are not going to have to testify. My hope is Stephen doesn't have his defenses up.

"It's well worth the risk. Good work, Logan. You've given me enough to go back into court and kick some ass."

***

McDermott begins the afternoon session by recalling Claude Bottoms for one more question.

"Mr. Bottoms, do you know a man named Christopher Slatterly?"

"Objection, your honor," Zeller says mildly irritated.

Before the judge can rule, McDermott interjects: "I can tie it in with my next witness, your honor."

"Then I will allow it. Answer the question, Mr. Bottoms."

"Yes, sir."

"In what capacity, please?"

"Chris was my cellmate until he was paroled a few months ago."

"Would you describe him as a close, personal friend?"

"We knew each other well enough, I suppose. But I wouldn't say we're best friends or anything like that."

McDermott takes a deep breath and prepares himself for the witness who will make the case for the prosecution or break it wide open for the defense.

"I call Stephen Buckingham."

Stephen is caught off guard, as McDermott wanted. He looks surprised, perhaps startled before rising from his chair to be sworn in. McDermott notices Zeller putting his head together with two of his associates. They've undoubtedly been caught off guard as well.

"Mr. Buckingham, I am correct, am I not, in stating that you are the brother of the late Broderick Nathaniel Buckingham, and the brother-in-law of Maggie Buckingham?"

"I am Nat's brother and the *former* brother-in-law of the defendant," he sneers, staring straight at Maggie with all the contempt and hatred a look from one human being can communicate to another.

"I take it from your emphasis on the word 'former' that you dislike your *former* sister-in-law."

"You take that correctly, and then some!"

"May I presume the rest of your family as well as any number of other friends and associates are aware of your feelings?"

"I've made no secret of it."

"Your brother knew as well?"

"Nat knew how I felt before he married that woman against my better judgment and the judgment of my family as well. We all knew she married him for his name and his money. And after she got what she wanted, she treated him like so much dirt under her feet!"

To which, Judge McKnight asks: "Mr. McDermott, I'm surprised you are letting Mr. Buckingham's allegations go without a challenge. Am I to understand you have no objections?"

"I do not, your honor."

"Oh, well, then continue."

"Mr. Buckingham, are you familiar with Christopher Slatterly, a former cellmate of Claude Bottoms?"

"I know him, yes."

"Isn't it true that you have served as his defense attorney several times since he was arrested for embezzlement five years ago?"

"Yes, I was his defense counsel."

"Have you had any contact with Mr. Slatterly since he was paroled six months ago."

"I do not think so, but I would have to check my office records to be sure."

"No need for that, Mr. Buckingham. I have Mr. Slatterly's telephone records since he left prison, and they show one call from your office to his residence on April 22. Do you remember making that call?"

"No, but it could have been made by a staff member regarding a balance owed in his account."

"I presume you did know LeRoy Bottoms, Mrs. Buckingham's former husband."

"We had met on a couple of occasions, but I never really knew him or had the desire to."

"Do you know his brother, Claude?"

"No. Not before the trial."

"Mr. Buckingham, are you aware that two weeks after LeRoy Bottoms died and two days after a telephone call from your office to Christopher Slatterly that Mr. Slatterly visited Claude at the prison, and the very next day, Claude contacted the police and the prosecutor's office with his story linking Maggie Buckingham to the fifty thousand dollars and the murder?"

The howls of protest McDermott fully expected burst instantly from the prosecutor.

"Pure speculation, your honor. It's one of the cheap, dirty courtroom tricks Mr. McDermott is infamous for pulling. He needs to immediately provide proof positive or be held in contempt!"

"Objection sustained. Mr. McDermott," Judge McKnight says in the manner of an adult attempting to correct a habitually misbehaving child. "Get to your proof or cease this line of questioning immediately. Do you have proof, sir?"

"I have this witness from a family with limitless financial means and an intense hatred for Nat Buckingham's widow, and too many ties to

175

Claude Bottoms and Christopher Slatterly to be mere concidence, your honor."

"Then I order you to sit down, say not another word, and give Mr. Zeller his turn to question this witness."

Zeller knows McDermott has severely damaged his case by implication, inference, and, yes, his usual courtroom theatrics. He must do his best quickly to remove the suspicion jurors can't help having following McDermott's questions.

"Mr. Buckingham, the defense counsel, Mr. Gus McDermott, is, as the jurors can plainly judge for themselves, once again up to his customary sleight of hand, posing misleading questions as if they were irrefutable facts in the hope that the jurors will believe them. Therefore, Mr. Buckingham, I ask you to look directly into the eyes of each juror as you answer my only two questions to you: First, did you give fifty thousand dollars in cash to Christopher Slatterly to bury in Mrs. Dunkle's shed? And second, did you have Mr. Slatterly persuade Claude Bottoms to claim the money was paid by Maggie Buckingham to LeRoy Bottoms to kill her husband?"

"Absolutely not!"

And with those two words, testimony ended, and the judge set closing arguments for nine a.m. the next day.

Chapter Thirty-Eight

The Verdict

The closing arguments are anticlimactic. Both the defense and the prosecution present the points most favorable to their case, but nothing new or remarkable or mind-changing is said.

Neither side is totally confident. All they can do is sweat out the wait while the jurors make their decision.

Maggie, of course, wants reassurance. After all, twelve people will now decide whether she gets to walk out of court a free and very, very rich woman who can afford to go anywhere, buy virtually anything, and live any way she chooses. Or whether she will spend the next four decades or so in a six-by-eight-foot windowless room with bars on it.

Gus is convinced of several things. One, under the best of circumstances the jurors do not like Maggie. She is not the kind of person they want for a friend or a neighbor. But Gus does not believe they dislike her enough to send her to prison for that reason alone.

He also believes Willa Dunkle's testimony helped greatly. The jury obviously respects her for the good, God-fearing woman she is—a woman who would sacrifice her time and go into debt looking after a nephew who had lived a life of crime. When she said Claude Bottoms was lying, the jury had to believe her. She had no reason whatsoever to lie herself. LeRoy was dead; she couldn't do anything to help him. And she did say she'd like to see Claude get out of jail as soon as possible. But not enough to provide cover for his lies.

Gus also strongly believes he has made Stephen look "guilty as hell" on the witness stand. The jury had to see his startled look when he was summoned. And his attempt to make his relationship with Christopher

Slatterly seem so insignificant that it was forgettable obviously failed. No, Gus could not prove Stephen's direct connection to the money and the plot to implicate Maggie. But he had "blown enough smoke" to raise reasonable doubt, and if the jurors follow the judge's definition of reasonable doubt, how can they convict Maggie?

Zeller, on the other hand, is worried about the circumstantial nature of his evidence. But he is convinced he has made the jury believe Maggie cared little, if anything, about her husband and wanted out of her marriage, taking with her millions of dollars in Buckingham money. But did he convince them Maggie was willing to go so far as to have Nat killed to accomplish those ends?

Mostly, however, Zeller is depending on the defense's almost total lack of proof of Maggie's innocence. Just as Claude could not actually prove his allegations were true, the defense could not actually prove they were not.

The prosecutor is not convinced he can get a guilty verdict, but he does believe the worst outcome will be a hung jury, giving him a chance to either try the case over or get Maggie and McDermott to plead guilty to a lower charge like manslaughter.

Each side anxiously awaits the verdict.

***

Meanwhile, Maggie has gotten her spirit back. She is not going to stand to hear the verdict looking like a beaten woman. What the judge, the prosecutors, the jury, the spectators—and especially the photographers and television camera operators—see will be a spectacular-looking woman dressed as if she were having tea with the queen of England. Maggie will leave the courtroom either the best-dressed, most beautiful woman ever sent to prison from New River County or a free woman charming the media and beaming for an audience far and wide.

Maggie doesn't know it, but that image will be the first Olivia ever sees of her, too. Olivia is joining Forrest, and Belinda and her brother in court to hear the outcome. She is eager to get a good look at this woman who has so thoroughly affected the course of Forrest's life. Maybe seeing Maggie and Forrest in the same room at the same time will give her further insight into how he has become the man he is.

They won't have much longer to wait because the forewoman has notified the court the jury has come to a decision. Word reaches Belinda through an associate in McDermott's law firm, and they arrive in court fifteen minutes later.

The first person to greet them is McDermott himself, and, he, too, is outfitted for the cameras. His expensive dark blue suit is complemented by a flaming red bow tie and pocket handkerchief, and he looks as if he has just gotten his teeth whitewashed for the occasion.

"It's a good sign the jury came back in only two days," he assures everybody, but they think his optimism seems somewhat forced, and his words provide little comfort because the prosecutor, Adam Zeller, is also preened out in his running-for-governor best.

They take their seats as Maggie makes her grand entrance, drawing the oohs and ahhs she had envisioned. The bailiff calls for everyone to stand as Judge McKnight takes his seat, pounds his gavel, turns to the jury forewoman and asks (although he already knows the answer): "Has the jury reached a decision?"

"Yes, your honor," she says and hands the verdict to the bailiff who carries it to the judge. He reads it in the emotionless manner he perfected long ago and hands it back to the bailiff who returns it to the forewoman.

"The defendant will rise," Judge McKnight orders, and Maggie stands strongly, looking straight ahead and defiantly confident, even though she is numb with apprehension.

Belinda, Nat, Forrest, and Olivia wrap their arms around one another's waists and hold their collective breath.

"How do you find?" the judge asks.

The forewoman carefully opens the written verdict as if she is seeing it for the first time, tries in vain to calm herself, and says in a shaky but loud voice:

"We, the jury, find the defendant, Maggie Buckingham, *not guilty!*"

Chapter Thirty-Nine

Maggie and Olivia Size up Each Other

Gus McDermott is not a gracious winner. After hugging and congratulating a euphoric Maggie, he struts his way over to the jurors to thank each one individually while glancing over at the prosecutor's table to rub it in and make Adam Zeller's day even worse, if that's possible.

Zeller is wearing his *c'est la vie* expression and trying to vanish out a side door and let his underlings face the news media. He is crestfallen; the case has not provided the stepping stone he risked his career on but instead has proved to be a stumbling block to his aspirations for higher office.

"Not guilty" are now Maggie's two favorite words in the English language. She embraces everyone at the defense table, blows kisses to the jurors, waves wildly with both hands and arms at Belinda, Nat, Forrest, and Olivia, and then radiant with relief and joy, she allows the reporters, photographers, and TV camera operators to encircle her, smiling, laughing and answering all of their predictable questions.

The only downers for Maggie are the shouts of "you got away with murder" and "get out of town" from a few spectators walking past her on the courthouse steps. Maggie ignores them; nobody is going to spoil this day for her.

Nat's parents and siblings depart tearfully and with bitterness. It appears no one will "pay" for the murder of their loved one. LeRoy died from cancer after serving not a single day in jail. Maggie, who Nat's parents and sister are convinced hired LeRoy to rid her of her husband, can never be tried again for the murder. She will collect the ten million dollars in life insurance money, share millions more in inheritance money with her two children, and gain sole ownership of the splendid house paid for in full by Nat. There is nothing the family can do but seethe in anger and console themselves with Nat's most precious gift to them—their grandson.

Stephen Buckingham, however, may face a prison sentence of his own. McDermott, with the help of his investigator, Logan Fernsby, threw enough suspicion on him to warrant further investigation. Only Stephen and Christopher Slatterly know for sure whether they attempted to frame Maggie, but Adam Zeller is angry enough over his lost opportunity to want to make up for it, at least partly, by getting a conviction against somebody. And Stephen Buckingham is not just an ordinary "some-body"; he's from a family so prominent, so rich, and so powerful the media would have a field day reporting on such a case.

***

When Belinda is finally able to separate her mother from all the attention she is getting, they drive away in Belinda's car and head to Forrest's mansion where he has an informal celebratory dinner waiting. He had it prepared "just in case."

Maggie is surprised and has misgivings but is pleased to be the center of attention. As apprehensive as she was before the verdict, she still figured out the "extra woman" sitting with her children and Forrest had to be his lady friend. Maggie, being Maggie, is eager to observe and evalu-ate. It doesn't take long for these two intelligent women to come to conclusions.

Olivia understands almost immediately why men would stumble all over themselves around Maggie. She is good-looking and sexy, of course, but beyond all that, she has a "presence" about her. She is confident, very much at ease and seems not only to invite the attention she gets but also to flourish in it.

"Poor Forrest," Olivia concludes. "A grown man stands little chance of resisting her kind of temptation. When he was an adolescent, he stood none."

Yet, Olivia feels no jealousy, no rivalry. After what happened between her and Forrest at The Greenbrier, she is secure in their relationship. Forrest, she is certain, wants nothing to do with Maggie romantically; he has overcome his addiction. Olivia believes she can be in Maggie's company now and at future gatherings and events and be civil.

Maggie sees in Olivia a quality that has always eluded her. Olivia is not only a pretty, desirable woman, but more importantly she is admired. Maggie is not—not by her family, nor her friends, and certainly not by the large number of people who dislike her. Olivia, Maggie can easily tell, is poised, thoughtful, gracious, and wise. No one in any gathering is going to outthink or outmaneuver her. Although she is cheerful, friendly, and outgoing, Olivia runs her every word and action through her mind before she says or does anything. Maggie admires that because, although she herself is intelligent and cunning, she is not always under control and has paid dearly for it.

"One thing's for sure," Maggie concludes. "She's damn near perfect for Forrest. I'm going to have to have a little chat with this Chicago girl."

Pushing her chair away from the table, Maggie looks at Olivia, and says, "I'm heading for the 'little girls room.' Care to join me, Olivia?"

Olivia recognizes the hidden meaning and gets to her feet immediately, saying, "Sure." Something intriguing is up, and Olivia finds herself being surprisingly eager to know what it is.

The bathroom is some distance away from the table, so there is no possibility they will be overheard. Olivia wastes no words or time getting to the point. She is friendly enough, but the door had no sooner closed than Olivia mildly challenges Maggie. "I have a feeling you have something to tell me, Maggie?"

"Belinda told me you're smart, Olivia, and my instincts tell me she is right. Fact is, she has told me quite a bit about you. I have to admit I was a receptive audience because I wanted to know about this woman who can make Forrest think about marriage again.

"Look, Olivia. I'm not trying to interfere or give unsolicited advice or anything like that. I simply want to take this opportunity that I might not get again to tell you I'm glad for you and Forrest. You seem ideally suited for each other, and Lord knows he deserves all the happiness he can get after the hell I put him through. Believe me, if I could have seen into the future, I not only would have said 'I do' at the altar with Forrest, I would have prostrated myself and pledged my eternal love and gratitude."

Both women enjoy a brief chuckle as they picture such a sight in their mind's eye. "My point is this, Olivia: Marry him, and the sooner the better. After Belinda, who loves both of you dearly, no one will be happier about a marriage between you and Forrest than I. And be assured, you have nothing to fear from me. Your happy marriage will help me atone a little for all the wrong I did him. I sincerely wish only the best for you."

Without another word, the only two women Forrest has ever loved hug warmly and look a little more trustingly at each other.

"Is it all right if I take a turn at saying something now, Maggie?

"Sure, whatever you want."

"What are you going to do with your life now? Can you be happy in Asher Heights with the hostility Nat's family and quite a few others feel for you?"

"Good question, Olivia. I've been putting off any thoughts about that until after the trial. But now that I am free and clear of legal problems, I can make some decisions. Fortunately, like you and Forrest, I am very wealthy. I can afford to go wherever I want and do pretty much whatever I decide.

"My first thought is that a long trip would be advisable. That would give me plenty of time to consider how to undo some of the things I can still make amends for, and also try to follow my daughter's example of how to be a better person in general. After that, who knows?"

"Sounds to me like a good beginning, Maggie. Please know, our door —Forrest's and mine—is always open to you."

"Thank you, Olivia. Now I guess we'd better get back to the table," Maggie grins, "before people start wondering how we could spend so much time together in a bathroom."

Chapter Forty

"What about the Rest of Your Life, Forrest?"

A few weeks after the trial has faded into the background and the attention of Asher Heights residents is focused on other matters, Belinda figures the time is right for her to nudge Forrest to face some decisions he has been conveniently ignoring. Nobody else seems willing to do it, so she appoints herself.

"Now what?" Belinda asks Forrest as they have coffee and doughnuts while sitting side-by-side on barstools amid all the shiny chrome and neon lights in his basement soda shop.

"Now what, what?" Forrest questions back. "What are you being nosy about with that suspicious little grin on your face?"

"What are you going to do next, Forrest? Your fabulous mansion is finished and it's the talk of the town. You and mother have finally come to terms, and now that she's packed up all her millions and is island-hopping throughout the southern hemisphere, she's totally out of your life. You've made Olivia gushingly happy. And you've run out of projects. You're not going to just sit around and work crossword puzzles, are you?"

"You know, for a young woman who was so meek and respectful around me when we first got to know each other, you've gotten to be downright cheeky lately."

"And you love me that way, admit it."

"Sure as hell do," he retorts, knowing how Belinda frowns upon even the mildest forms of swearing.

"Answer my questions, *Mister Alderson,*" she orders in mock politeness.

"I don't know what I'm going to do next. I put half a lifetime of planning into what I just finished. Never occurred to me to think beyond that. Aren't I entitled to a break before you guilt me back into doing something more productive?"

"Sure, take another week," she chides. "I have some suggestions if you'd like to hear them?"

"I'm listening. Let's hear how you've been planning my life for me, Belinda."

"A foundation for one thing, Forrest. I know your conscience won't give you any peace if you hoard all your money for yourself. So why not set up a foundation, let Olivia operate it, and put me in charge of locating the worthy people and organizations we should help. I'm willing to put my money where my mouth is, too, considering my wonderful stepfather loved me so much he left me several million dollars."

"Tell you what, Belinda. I like your idea and I think you're ideally suited for the role you've carved out for yourself. Besides," he winks, "now that you're 'Miss Moneybags' yourself, I wouldn't have to worry about you embezzling from me.

"But why Olivia? She's a partner in a huge Chicago law firm, and although I am fully confident she could do a bang up job of running a foundation, what makes you think she'd give up her position to do it? Have you two been conspiring behind my back?"

"Nope. Having Olivia run the foundation is simply another part of *The Plan* I have for your life."

"How's that, Belinda? You lost me somewhere along the way."

"Let me put it this way," she beams, giving Forrest her most mischievous look. Then she sings, "Dah dah dee dum, dah dah dee dum, dah dah dee dah, dah dah dah dah dee dum," and ends with a fit of laughter.

"Oh, very amusing!"

"C'mon, Forrest. You know you love her. And I know for certain she loves you. It's written plain in big, bold headline type all across her face, especially whenever you're in the same room. You are going to marry her, aren't you?"

"And just how is that any of your business, Miss Impudent?"

"Because I love both of you and both of you love me. Simple as that. Now answer me because you know I'm going to pester you until you do?"

"Well, if it will get you off my back, I'll admit it. Yes, I love Olivia. And we're headed for marriage, I think. And that's all I'm saying on that subject. You finished?"

"Almost. We still have to decide what *you* are going to do. Olivia and I, with some hired help, can run the foundation without any interference from you. We just need for you to fork over the money. As for you, I think you should be a college professor."

"A college professor!" Forrest interrupts loudly. "Are you nuts! Besides, I only have a bachelor's degree. Most professors have a Ph.D. or at least a master's degree. I don't think they hire anyone with just a bachelor's."

"Are you kidding, Forrest? Are you forgetting who you are? Remember what someone at the University of Cincinnati said when another person mentioned that astronaut Neil Armstrong was the only full professor of aerospace engineering there without a Ph.D? He had the perfect comeback. He said Armstrong was also the only full professor who had ever walked on the moon. Well, you'd be the only professor in the business school who had started with nothing and amassed almost a billion dollars in personal wealth.

"Forrest, all you have to do is arrange an appointment with the dean of the business program at Concord, Bluefield State, West Virginia Tech, or Marshall or any other good college or university in southern West

Virginia, offer them a big donation and tell them you're willing to teach for a dollar a semester."

Forrest breaks up with laughter. "You're overestimating me in several ways, Belinda. First, even if they'd hire me, I don't know if I'd be any good at it. Second, I don't want to be bogged down with a full-time job. Third, it can snow anytime between November and the end of March, and I'm not interested in commuting in icy weather."

"Way ahead of you, Forrest. Why not teach one semester a year, preferably the second semester from January into the first half of May. You could teach two classes that meet Tuesdays and Thursdays and one night class on Wednesdays. That would leave you free from Friday through Monday every week for you and Olivia to go wherever you want."

"And how, my friend, have you figured out how to beat the winter weather?"

"Simple, Forrest. You're super rich. Buy or rent a nice, cozy place in the town of whichever college you teach for, and you can live there three days a week when necessary. Olivia could stay with you. Any foundation business that didn't require her presence could be done by computer."

"OK, I give in. I'll think about giving that a go. Actually, four of the happiest years of my life were spent on a college campus. I loved being around a bunch of smart young people, going to the Artist Series programs, and, as far as I'm concerned, there's no better way to spend a crisp, sunny Saturday afternoon than sitting among a bunch of fired-up students at a football game.

"Any other bright ideas before I get on with my day, Belinda?"

"Maybe one other that's only half-baked so far, but I think it has merit. This mansion is too glorious for just you and Olivia and your family and small circle of friends. Why not have a Visitors Day on a regular basis and give everybody a chance to experience this place? You could have a donation box at the end of the tour and give the money to the foundation or some other worthy cause.

"Then, too, it seems a shame to leave that beautiful chapel unused most of the time. In addition to you and Olivia getting married in it, why not make it available for other couples, choosing them on the basis of merit, like those who have performed noteworthy public service, or volunteered a significant amount of time to senior citizens centers, or have kept litter off the roadways? The possibilities are endless."

"If I did, would you be willing to take charge of and responsibility for those projects and any others you dream up, Belinda?"

"Oh, gosh yes, Forrest. I mean, I've been joking some this afternoon, but seriously, most of what we've been discussing is truly doing God's work. And that's what I'd dearly love having the privilege to do for the rest of my life."

"Well, you know even better than I do it's obvious I've become a pushover for you, Belinda. Whatever you want. Just run it by me first.

"Now, how about a grilled cheese sandwich and some iced tea?"

Chapter Forty-One

Forrest Surprises Boyhood Friends

Forrest has been saving a get-together with his boyhood buddies until a surprise he has planned for them is finished to the finest detail. He has told no one about it; in fact, he has gone to a lot of trouble and considerable expense to keep it a secret.

And now he is ready for the big event, so he invites them and their families for hot dogs and hamburgers in his fifties basement soda shop and a tour of the mansion. But a meal and a tour are just an excuse to get the guys together.

So he has conspired with Belinda to lead the women and the children on a tour while he quietly rounds up his boyhood pals—Whitney Rutherford, Chris Mathis, Sandy Overmeyer, and Stretch Maddox—and shuffles them out a side door to what appears to be some unfinished construction.

It looks like one of those portable tents dedicated tailgaters put up on Saturday mornings before a big afternoon college football game, only it is much larger. But instead of entering the tent, Forrest signals to a crew of men he has hired to take the coverings down.

He holds his breath, looking at his friends' faces instead of what is being unveiled, so hopeful his surprise will have as much meaning to the other guys as it does to him.

"Ho-ul-lee shit!" Whitney yells in delight, laughing so hard he can barely get his next words out. "It's my old basketball court! Damn, Forrest, it's an exact replica. Even the goal and backboard are relics of the past. It's even in the same location. How in the world did you manage that?"

"With a lot of scheming and a whole lot of pieces of green paper with presidents' faces on them. I don't know where the people I hired found all this stuff, but here it is, and all of it is genuine."

After all the whooping and hollering following the unveiling, Stretch says, "All we need now is a basketball. Didn't forget that, did you, Forrest?"

Right on cue, one of the workers moves his hand from behind his back and displays a shiny, never-used-before, fresh-out-of-the-box basketball made in 1952 and locked away in a storehouse for decades.

Stretch takes it in both of his big slim hands and gets the feel of it. Then he dribbles it expertly while the others watch in amazement.

"Don't be too impressed," Stretch grins. "I've been conducting clinics for school kids ever since I retired from the pro leagues. That's why I haven't lost the touch. Now, let's see if ya'll have any skill left over from our glory days. Must say, though, that from the looks of you, we'll have to change the name of the fast break to the fat break."

"Think so, do you, Stretch?" Chris challenges. "There may be a little more of me than way back when, but I can still kick your skinny butt in a game of Horse any day. Got a Ben Franklin in my billfold to back it up."

"Hold on, guys," Forrest wades in, waving his arms toward his body to call everybody together. "I have a plan that will help us determine who's still got it, and I made sure it has nothing to do with who's in the best shape, knowing damn good and well none of us could go two or three hours the way we did when we were kids.

"We're going to have a shoot-around like the pros do every year before the NBA all-star game. Here's how it works. We're each going to take four shots from five different places I've already marked on the court. That's twenty shots with a time limit of two minutes. Sandy, you're first; Chris, second; Whitney, third; I'm fourth; and Stretch, last."

"How much money we gonna put up?" Stretch asks with the cockiness of a certain winner.

"Let me answer that," Sandy insists. "Because Stretch figures he can't be beat, let's have him put up a hundred and the rest of us twenty each. With all the expensive cars he sells every month, he can afford it."

"Done," they all agree.

Workers wheel out five racks, each containing four basketballs, and the guys go through their warm-ups and practice shots. Everybody except Stretch is obviously rusty, but nobody has completely forgotten how it's done, proving there's no age limit on memories. The thrill of athletic competition rekindles in their middle-aged bodies, and they manage to put everything else aside and lose themselves in the moment.

Their reunion offers a brief time out in which dates, ages, cares, worries, and the myriad pressures and demands of adult living fade out of consciousness. For right here and right now, Forrest and his boyhood buddies are back on that old hard-surface court trading challenges and good-natured sarcastic taunts, just as they did so long ago . . . in the shadow of Old Mrs. Kimble's Mansion.

On Sale Now!

**For more information
visit:** www.SpeakingVolumes.us

On Sale Now!

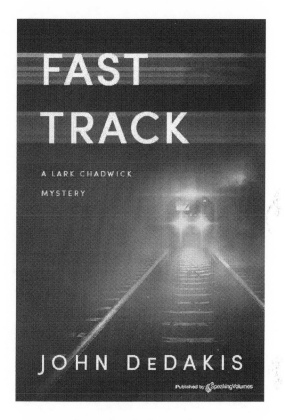

For more information
visit:

On Sale Now!

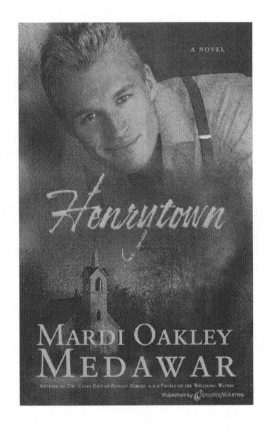

For more information
visit: www.SpeakingVolumes.us

Made in the USA
Middletown, DE
12 January 2021